TRAVELLERS MAY STILL RETURN

TRAVELLERS MAY STILL RETURN

MICHAEL KENYON

thistledown press

Thistledown Press Ltd.
410 2nd Avenue North
Saskatoon, Saskatchewan, S7K 2C3
www.thistledownpress.com

Library and Archives Canada Cataloguing in Publication
Title: Travellers may still return / Michael Kenyon.
Names: Kenyon, Michael, 1953- author.
Description: Short stories.
Identifiers: Canadiana (print) 20190131357 | Canadiana (ebook)
20190131764 | ISBN 9781771871877
(softcover) | ISBN 9781771871884 (HTML) | ISBN 9781771871891 (PDF)
Classification: LCC PS8571.E67 T73 2019 | DDC C813/.54—dc23

Cover painting, *West of Flight*, by Lorraine Thomson
Cover and book design by Jackie Forrie
Printed and bound in Canada

Canadä

Canada Council
for the Arts
Conseil des Arts
du Canada

cultivating
the arts

Thistledown Press gratefully acknowledges the financial assistance of
the Canada Council for the Arts, the Saskatchewan Arts Board, and the
Government of Canada for its publishing program.

ACKNOWLEDGEMENTS

Thanks to the fine people at Thistledown. Special thanks to Seán Virgo, brilliant editor, traveller of travellers.

In memory of Tom Clifford Kenyon

CONTENTS

Eros does not lead upward only but downward into that uncanny dark world of Hecate and Kali.

CG Jung

THE PREHISTORY OF JESSE GREEN

for the marriage of the Lamb has come,
and his Bride has made herself ready;
it was granted her to clothe herself
with fine linen, bright and pure.

Revelation 19:7-8

She was crazy she was not she was beautiful and rich she knew Miami meant my friend or my soul that's why we went there and lived in a hotel like tourists though it wasn't the destination just a place to rest and relate she said soul mates find out what's after friendship and her eyes lit up when she told me and I wanted nothing else but to go with her wherever even Panama she was so serious I got serious too after all it was an easy decision for me that spring sitting on a bench on Cornwall in Vancouver looking at water freighters high-rises trees mountains snow sky and her green eyes mostly her eyes and when the jay landed in the maple tree over the fence and chattered everything slowed down and it was the sign she said that we should stop talking and go

1.

"Chucha! Qué sopá?"

At first I could only see a silhouette, then the figure turned its head and I saw Jesus on the veranda outside the door, his terrified face grinning and nodding at a tall guy who spoke to him from the top of the stairs. "Tell me what's been found. Who has been here?"

Jesus laughed aloud and shrugged his shoulders. The moon was still up. That hissing was rain coming back or wind rattling the leaves, and the tops of the trees waved in a white wind and two lights shone from across the track, lanterns swaying slightly, or the moon reflecting on a vehicle, not yet, the road wasn't finished. Jesus's thin shoulders shrugged again under his gleaming shirt, how nervous he was. The man behind him was still talking, his voice low, one arm resting on the thick round rail. He'd come through the jungle or from the sea looking for us, and darkness jumped, a microscope lens cracking a slide, and their heads were together for a long time, night air singing around them, then first rain hit the roof, drowning out the wind in the estate's fields, and I kneeled on my bunk, trying to see Jesse in the huge hammock by the window, but Sucre's bulk was all I could make out, rolling in sleep, and her skinny hammock hanging loose beside his. "Jesse." No answer. For six months I've woken scared that she's been spirited away by a gangster, a gang of punks, in Vancouver, in Miami, any place between, in Panama City. No, no. She was in Sucre's hammock, squished under him. Easy as locks in the canal.

Around dawn I started to shake and soldiers were in the shadows, the ones who'd rescued us from police who'd held us on drug charges near the harbour, the young officer asking over and over who was our favourite rock-and-roll band, Jesse thin and wild, her clothes rags. "I know very well that you have rich friends here." The covered truck all over again through the deep green tunnel to the ugly pile of roots.

The fever lasted the whole day, events circling with the mosquitoes outside the gauze, the net, the gauze, the net, finally let up as darkness fell, and I walked around the compound and ate a bunch of tortillas and got buzzed on maté. Light as a feather, hollow as a reed. Screeching night birds and animals splashing in the tide-filled forest kept me back-checking, feet planted in mud at the beginning of the new road, for a long time, and I saw a silver coin, Mother Magda's face, in the trees. When she stepped out, her naked body was all scarred up, except the skin between her belly button and her blonde fur, which seemed pure and vast as a desert. When she turned I was freaked to see she had a short thick fleshy tail.

Late that night, after Sucre had gone to sleep, Jesse quit his hammock to join me in my narrow cot against the back wall of the house and we listened to the tide seeping out of the swamp. "It's salt crystals drying in the moonlight," she whispered. "It's killing the crops." And she's right. Each day the corn turns blacker and blacker while Sucre sits on his big stinking earth-mover and digs his dumb road past the cemetery to the old port so he can go fetch the owner's new car and take Jesse dancing. When I told her about the tall man on the veranda the night before, she laughed.

"It's only Jesus and a lover," she said. "Just get your strength back, okay? Don't waste your energy."

"Maybe it was the owner," I said.

"It's under control," she said. "Absolute control. We are totally safe."

"How do you know, Jesse?"

"Just we'd know if Pedrarias was here. Sucre would tell us. It's common sense. And when he sees me, he'll want to fuck me. You know something, Kenneth? If he comes before the road's finished I'll get him to fire Sucre. We'll be okay." She moved a fraction away from me, as far as she could in the slender space, and I could see her eyes. Something in me crouched. She always creates this little gap between us so I can see her body or some detail of it, and often, if I'm quiet, something happens, some deep agreement. The little fox in me woofed and nodded.

"How did it go today?" I asked.

She reached between my legs. "We're way past the cemetery. This is crazier than any place we've been. It's really wild, you know? There's something trying to happen. Feel it?"

"Yeah." I watched her face. "You fucked Sucre all day?"

"We worked on the road. Sucre's crazy about the road. He thinks it is cool that a man can build a road through jungle all by himself. Sometimes his bucket hits these buried rocks and roots and — " She paused, her fingers teasing. "He likes me to ride on his thigh, so when he's finished a hard bit he can shut off the engine and lift me onto his cock . . . "

"He does that?"

"Yeah."

Every leaf glimmered out beyond the veranda. In the mangrove, black water reflected the moon. The clamour of insects got muffled. I zipped my fingers across the netting. Cold flat light filled the land. The villagers were all sleeping.

"Jesse?"

"What?"

"When are we leaving?"

"Soon," she said. "The road's through, you know, almost ready. He's going to steal Pedrarias's car right off the freighter."

"I know."

"Pedrarias, he's rich. Way richer than my parents. He paid off the army. Sucre says his family's been ripping off peasants for generations. And Sucre's gonna rip off Pedrarias. It's like a showdown. He's like a rebel. We just need to be patient a bit longer."

She told me to go to sleep and slipped out of the bunk. I pulled the netting closed. She padded back to Sucre's hammock. A bird shrieked once. The big hammock rocked and creaked as the banker's daughter, Jesse Green, rode the rebel manager and made the same noises I'd heard her make to settle a horse.

It is true, I guess, that we've escaped, farther than I imagined possible, out of North America, beyond deep stuff like material and morals and ethics and safe sex, yet I'm still seventeen, Jesse's still nineteen, and the manager's a mean fat clueless son of a bitch. Jesse says we've come from the tits of the continent down to the cunt and we're *home*, but the word's a bubble, a tough clay marble, like the first pure ones she made in the college kiln. I'm scared though, same kind of scared as in my father's barn after dusk, my father. All I used to have to do. Remember Jesse's mouth that first time, remember the swallows over tall yellow grass, remember her in the hayloft before we cut loose. One night I counted seven times that Sucre fucked her.

I woke after midday, not a trace of fever, and lay in the bunk, curled up, listening for the distant machine pounding. Nothing. They'd be in the next valley, beyond the convent ruins. There was a thick smell in the room. My intestines struggled. The rain had stopped. I was very hungry and my bladder was full, so I pulled on jeans and a T-shirt and went out into the yard. Women from the shacks were cooking flatbread on a dull metal sheet over the open fire; the black urn simmered with beans. The women didn't look at me. I pissed behind a tree. Over the little hill rose a thick column of smoke. Parrots swooped from the mangroves to the jungle, lighting briefly on the roof of the manager's house, before taking off over the owner's villa, all shuttered, perched on a small rise above the little village. Jesus was with the women, speaking sharply. They gestured at me. They handed him a plate, which he brought over.

We stood together, Jesus bowing and grinning, while I scooped beans into my mouth. He mimed the bulldozer, his body jogging up and down.

"How are you, Ken?"

"Good."

"How is Jesse today?"

"Very good," I said.

"The road is nearly finished. Nearly perfect."

"So I hear. Mr Pedrarias will return soon?"

"You want water now?" He ran to the well. Parrots yammering in the trees behind him. The women laughing. In the time it took for him to bring the canteen, sun had broken through the clouds and the intensity of the green blew me away. A dog crawled out from under the veranda and flopped by the well.

I gulped from the canteen, biting the brackish water, challenging each mouthful to make me sick. "Mr Pedrarias, when will he arrive?"

Jesus looked around, wringing his hands. "When the car comes from Italy," he said. "That black very cool car, man. Very famous car. When the road is finished, Mr Pedrarias will drive the car out of the ship and all the way here. All the way from the city, man."

"Won't the road have to be graded?"

"He is loco." Jesus glanced at the villa, then opened his hands, his eyes wide. "He comes on the estancia once, twice a year by helicopter. He will kill that car. But you and Jesse." He laughed. "You and Jesse, man! You are the chosen! And the new car, of course, of course. All together."

"Mr Sucre says he will drive the car."

"Sucre fucks boys, girls, animals, no matter! He can't fuck a car. He counts this much." He pinched thumb and forefinger together, frowning. "Don't worry. I tell you a big secret. The road will change everything. Next year Mr Pedrarias will fire Sucre and get bored of his car and bored of you, you will go home, and I will be manager and fill in the mangrove and make good pasture."

"After the road."

"Yes. After the road. Yes. It is beautiful, no?" His body tilted. He held his arms wide. And I saw us from the air, two guys in a clearing, the blue ocean on one side, jungle forever, a state-of-the-art bulldozer in the next valley tearing a narrow rough cut in the ground. "It is beautiful, of course, like you. In the swimming pool that first day, you are white angels, like beautiful nuns, yes. Like nuns." He crossed himself. "Like nuns. Yes."

"Jesus, who was that man on the veranda two nights ago?"

"No man. There was no man."

"He spoke to you."

"No, you are wrong." He backed away across the dirt into the shadow of the wooden stairs. "You should not walk alone in the cemetery or in the fields. You should not walk in the mangrove or the ruins. You risk everything."

"Tell Jesse, not me."

"Because of the dead and because of the living. Because of Magda."

Just then the village men appeared along the rough road. Silently, they squatted before the cook fires, and the women ladled beans from the big pot into brown clay bowls and the men peeled flatbread from the hot metal with their fingers, swallowed it steaming with mouthfuls of dark beans. They reached for the water vessel, ran wet fingers through their hair.

Inside the house it was dark, though the sun still shone on the country around. Flies in the centre of the room kept changing direction. My face in the small mirror looked way young, like a foetus. A week ago Sucre had worked his bulldozer too close to the cemetery and pronged an old skeleton, face up, jaw gone. Then, close to the burn clearing, well clear of the cemetery, he'd unearthed some tiles, shards and more old skulls. I sat on the floor and kept watch through the screen door. The men finished their meal and went back to their cluster of shacks for siesta. Several of them peered up at the house without stopping their slow conversations. After a while, children and young women arrived from somewhere and the place filled with shouts and laughter. A young mother clutching her baby climbed the veranda stairs. I'd spoken to her a few days ago. She was nice. She stood in the doorway and said she had something she would like to sell, would I buy this thing from her.

The curved clay whistle was brown-red, evenly fired, and hard. On it was a raised design.

The woman's eyes followed my fingers as they traced the serpent's forked tongue. When I raised it to my lips, the baby's head fell back, then forward onto her breast, mouth fastening on her nipple. Rain poured from the sky, beating everything, then stopped. The children raced from the shacks to leap into the new puddles. The sound was thin and wavering. The woman's eyes, close to mine, were as dark and brown as the dark brown serpent's outline.

"Where did you get it?" I whispered, closing my fingers on the warm clay, stroking it.

"From the new road," she said. Her breath smelled like limes.

"It's old," I said. "And smooth, like skin."

She cupped her hand over the baby's head. "The tide is coming," she said. "Give me money. I must go."

I gave her some of Jesse's money. She tucked it into the front of her dress.

I smoked one of Sucre's cigarettes and watched wind ripple the edge of the jungle.

The mangroves turned red in the last sun. Sucre's earthmover rumbled over the hill toward the house. Through the cab's slanted windows I could see his hairy shoulders, the muscles in his back straining. The weight of his belly pulled him forward as he stepped down from the cab and strode through the muddy yard. The cook fires, rekindled after the rain, were burning fiercely, and he took the food the women gave him without slackening his pace. He set the bowls on the outside table and came in to wash. "Where's Jesse?" he growled.

"I thought she was with you."

"No."

I felt a trickle of fear, electric, along my spine, as I watched him scrub sweat and dirt from his upper body. My shoulders tensed and my fingers curled into fists. After washing, he walked over and slapped my face and I fell back against the cot, my eyes filling with water. When they cleared, Jesse was framed in the doorway. She looked numb, closed. Sucre grinned at her, helped me to my feet, and the three of us went out to the veranda. He yelled for Jesus to bring beer and we sat together drinking, watching the fires and the bloody moonrise. Smoke still billowed from the hill. He picked up the whistle, turned it over, studying the serpent. "What is this?"

"Mine. I found it."

I was terrified he was going to accuse me of something. Or hurl the whistle away. "I am tired," he said. He set the serpent on the reed table. "We will sleep."

2.

One day last spring I saw a fifty-dollar bill flying in the rainy wind on Robson Street and no one else seemed to notice but a beautiful girl, and I kneeled there, the soggy bill in my hand, and breathed in this small dark intense being who carried herself like a warrior, and she helped me spend the money.

She was eighteen and had slept with tons of men. She wasn't smarter than me, but she knew more about sex. We used the condo her parents paid for or we used her car or we used my parents' barn. The farmhouse was out of bounds because of my sister in her wheelchair, my mother always pushing her along the hallways, and Dad's ghost which, when it wasn't haunting the horses in the pasture that belonged to the neighbour now, hung out drinking in one room or another. Jesse Green was into tats and piercings and crack and ecstasy, pushing herself at different obnoxious men, which I didn't understand until it dawned on me that she loved testing her immunity to worship, admiration, cruelty, deviousness. And then one day she said she would quit drugs, alcohol, coffee, and would not fuck around, at all, ever, if I promised to go away with her. She'd been in and out of institutions and rehabs since she was twelve. Her parents, a banker and a psychologist, supported her from Calgary. She'd gone to school in England and now was registered at Emily Carr College of Art but never attended classes, needed only access to the kiln, where she'd fire different-sized variegated clay balls, and to be near the ocean, wandering Kits beach or the sea wall. "We'll get lost in the summer," was her phrase, and, "Keep me on track," as we tried to switch from crack to crystal meth. She wore this cool kind of amazing protective, maybe inherited, kind of wild friendliness that intensified the reactions of those around her, to lust of course, but also confusion. Guys hitting on her often stalled as if the signals she was sending were impairing their lines and angles. I saw desire lines everywhere in Vancouver. She acted outrageous to bend light. She made everything equal and talked fast. It was hard to understand and impossible to know where things were going but everything seemed solid state, like no gaps between things, then no things at all.

I'd skip school and hitchhike from Pit Meadows into town and we'd fuck all day long in her condo, then read bits from books to each other. The fucking was like a star collapsing, or maybe the universe. Or she'd drive out to the farm and we'd borrow the neighbour's horses and ride, the rush-hour traffic streaming alongside, the stag leaping across the road into swaying black firs a warning, she said, that any crazy moment might uproot trees and unscrew signs from poles and we'd be forever suburbanite ghosts. We were okay, she said, but danger existed. She got herself hired for a few weeks on the neighbour's farm, and we rode and talked a lot, on and on, galloping and horny, and afterward we melted down in the old barn, poured ourselves out. The more we did the more she demanded, and I really didn't want to be anywhere without her. There wasn't anywhere that wasn't her. That's the truth.

Jesse Green was seriously moody when she was stoned on grass, and once we were lying on loose hay at sunset, watching bats twitching from the rafters and swallows swinging in and out the high barn door, and we hadn't spoken for hours, when she said, in her faint English accent, "I'm upside down, I'm fucked," and I stared into those green eyes amid the chaos of Dad's barn and saw what she really was, and what I really was and promised her I'd go anywhere with her, though I didn't believe for a second that there was anywhere to go. And I said so.

"You're full of shite," she said.

And the sun set red over the fields, the west sky, and she said we'd go, soon now, she'd take me.

I didn't want any kind of change. We were eternal and boundless and we toked meth and I told the accident story and she zigged and zagged. She said she was done with crack and almost done with crystal meth and was pretty sure of getting off the oxy. That's when the little fox was born, just a pup, inside me. I remember thinking about a world where all things might be variations, everything a version of the same ripple, and I hadn't crashed the car in Nowhere, Alberta on my fifteenth birthday because Mom and Dad were too drunk to drive, pushing the gas, pushing the car out of control, and no one was dead at all, though my face was cut up, and the others seemed dead, all of them, till doctors brought my mom and sister back. And the sky would still be the same, the world just as safe or unsafe, everything the same, but I would see it differently. I've been back to the stretch of prairie highway a few times, different seasons, times of day, and there must be a defect under the road, a geological fault of some kind, because the land buckles on either side, and the gravel of the soft shoulder makes a wave, and despite the repair jobs there is always a new crack next to the holes already filled with tarmac, a new gap waiting to be filled, a cave where some creature might live, and I always crouch to peer in and see dust and darkness, and once I saw the small bones of a dry bird. And because in the old world my mother was barely alive and my father was dead and my sister in a wheelchair I loved Jesse infinitely, though I didn't want sex nearly as much as she did, and because of all this, the fifty bucks, the accident, the drugs, the fox cub, the world became an enormous, undifferentiated place. And there was nothing to escape, and that gave us the escape velocity.

3.

Just daylight when he got up, when Sucre got up, and even though I felt sick, the way I always feel in the morning, I got up too and sat on the bunk and watched him dress in the grungy clothes he'd taken off last night, watched him heat water on the oil stove out on the veranda, pick his nose as he cooked cornmeal, and when he brought a bowl to Jesse, I slipped out the back and threw up. Sky gleamed slate blue. The sun would soon show, after the rain, and the heat would be a weight on our heads. I dipped my cup into the rain barrel. The village women on their way to the swamp, red and brown woven bags tied empty at their waists, sang and whistled as they climbed over roots toward the receding sea to collect mussels. I dropped the lid onto the half-full barrel. Back inside, Jesse was peering from the hammock at Sucre boiling his thick oily coffee in the same pot he'd cooked the meal. I felt like my old man's ghost as I drifted through the room, back to front, and sat in one of the cane chairs. Beyond the veranda, men stood around and smoked, then wandered in a group up to the farm fields. Small children chased chickens. The eternal feeling was still with me — I could touch it: the women to the sea, men to the fields, children dashing in circles, us in the middle. The young woman who'd sold me the serpent whistle had just slaughtered a little pig at the bottom of the veranda steps. She smiled up, her fingers full of blood. She wasn't much older than Jesse.

Sucre grunted, catching me looking. "You're a dog," he said. "That one's already taken. She's got a hard-working husband and a baby. You're a lazy dog. You should work with the others." He gestured past the shacks to the fields and the black jungle.

"Can I ask you a question?" I said.

He banged his cup against the wall of the house and wet black grounds fell through the boards of the veranda. "No," he said. Then he laughed. "Okay. Today I will permit you a question." I flinched when he moved, quickly for a fat man, and snatched the clay whistle from my fingers. "What will you do with this?"

"Nothing."

The platform rocked as he crashed down the stairs. He tossed the piece back and shouted,. "Ask me your question tonight. If I don't like your question I'll fuck you. That's the end of it."

Jesse came out and we watched him mount his cab. The machine rattled into life and she shuddered.

"Let's see what you got," she said.

I held out the whistle. "Some kind of really old pottery. Where were you yesterday?"

"Up at the ruins." She leaned against my shoulder and turned the piece to the light. "Where'd you get it?"

"A girl from the village sold it to me. Some kind of snake whistle. It's cool isn't it?"

"Where'd you get the money?"

"Your stash."

"It has horns."

"You're not going with him?"

"Of course I'm going." She raced after Sucre's machine, feet spraying mud, parrots in flight, and climbed on. After a moment, the bulldozer plunged into the jungle.

I lay on the day hammock, listening to rain hammering the roof. Around noon it stopped and I heard the rotors of a chopper louder and louder then deafening. Trees to the west were bending and waving, then the glass-and-metal dragonfly spun up out of the forest and the scream faded away. A man in a filthy white suit slithered down the slope of the new road to the yard, circled the compound, glancing into the huts and up at the house. I slipped out of the hammock to the shadow of the overhang. Across the yard the huts were steaming. My fingers recognised and recognised the whistle, the snake, in the front pocket of my jeans. This was a new strand, maybe good, on its way. This was the same man I'd seen with Jesus the other night.

Maybe it wasn't him, but it was a similar tall guy wearing glasses, and he was carrying a large leather bag, and he looked two dimensional in the hot sun. Tears were coming. Why? *Because I'm trapped, because I'm lonely. Because I'm homesick.* I was ashamed of my appearance. I hadn't washed in days. I took out the whistle and the snake uncoiled its length to fill the thick clay. I set it down on the outside table, rinsed my face in the rain barrel, pulled on my ball cap, and leaned out over the veranda railing.

"I am looking for the manager!" the man called.

"Sucre?"

"Of course. That's his name. Yes." He was maybe thirty, and self-assured as he stepped carefully round the puddles and placed a foot on the veranda's lowest step, one hand on the rail. "Who are you?" His expensive boots shone where they were not muddy.

"My name is Kenneth." I held out my hand. "Kenneth Doblin."

"I am Berman." His fingers slipped through mine, and he slid past me and peered into the dark house. "You are alone?"

"I've been ill."

"Ah. And you are not from here." He was close, his face right in front of me. He smelled sweet. I leaned against the doorjamb and closed my eyes and sweat ran down my back, soaked into the splintery wood. "Do you know what you are?"

"What?"

"You are a beautiful young man." He took from his leather bag a bowl with a round bottom and a wide rim. The bowl, more than a foot in diameter, was cracked and bruised in places. He held it to me, sharing something secret. "Do you know what this is?"

"A big bowl." I touched the heavy chipped rim. Two circles, thick black lines, followed the edge. Black etched columns divided the outer surface into panels. The glaze was an ochre colour, and the exposed clay along the cracks where the glaze had flaked was rich red.

"No, not a bowl. Not a bowl."

He likes boys. He likes me. We were close together, in the same places as Jesus and he had stood nights ago. Bloody footprints on the steps from the murdered pig. Sunlight through a hole in the overhang cut across his stark figure in the middle of the veranda. He was looking at the reed table.

"Do you know where you are?"

"The Pedrarias Estate."

"This was found recently, Mr Doblin." He turned the bowl, whatever it was, bottom up. "It's an urn cover. A burial urn. Very old." His lips were thick, babyish. Our hands touched the glaze. An electronic beep went off and he slid the urn, whatever, back into his satchel, sat at the outside table and flipped open his phone. "Chucha . . . the connection is shit. Do you have a land line?"

"When the road is finished. So they say. Mr Sucre keeps the satellite phone locked up."

"Shit. Could I have a drink of water?"

I filled two cups at the rain barrel and we sipped water, watching the women and boys return with their bags of mussels from the mangrove. The boys stopped to look at us. I called Jesus to bring food.

"Are you travelling alone, Mr Doblin?"

Berman's back was almost straight and his thick hair glistened like anthracite. He lit a cigarette. Stood, smoking, looking out. I couldn't trust him, but felt like explaining that we were prisoners.

"With my girlfriend . . . "

Jesus returned with plates of rice and coconut and sugar cane. He and Berman did not react to each other. We sat down to eat.

"You're American," he said at last.

"Canadian," I said.

A slight smile. "We both have German names. We were once countrymen, yes? When will the manager be back?"

"In a while. Always before dark."

After we'd eaten I fetched two bottles of cold beer from the cooler and he offered me a cigarette.

"I'm with the university," he said. "From the university. Mr Pedrarias is building a road and he disturbs some graves. What is disturbed interests us." He picked up the clay whistle from the table. "Like this, Mr Doblin."

"It's mine. I bought it."

"Is that right? Can you tell me, Mr Doblin, who you bought this from?"

"A woman."

"And where did she get it?"

"She said it came from the new road."

"The new road."

"From the cemetery near the new road."

"This is too old to come from the cemetery. What exactly are you are doing here?"

"Waiting for the owner. We . . . I'm . . . "

"Ah, yes?" He sat upright, his boot tapping, impatient. "I don't believe you understand your situation, Mr Doblin." He swallowed the last of his beer, belched. "You know, that road will never be built now. These are important discoveries." He caressed his bag, stretched out his legs. "I'm very tired, Mr Doblin. I find myself unable to stay awake. I would like to lie down somewhere."

On my cot I dreamed it was morning and Jesse and Sucre were tangled in the big hammock. But no. Berman was still asleep in the outside hammock, his heavy satchel nestled between his legs.

I woke late in the afternoon. Berman was up and shaved, pacing the veranda. His boots, beside the water barrel, were spotless and sparkling.

"Perhaps you can point out the woman," he said. "The woman who found the serpent piece."

"That one over there," I said. "The woman with the baby."

He started down the steps, returned for his hat, then crossed the yard to the woman's shack. She looked up at him as he approached her, using a finger to turn a strand of black hair behind her ear. She stepped inside her doorway and he stood outside, beating his hat against the side of his leg. I felt like a betrayer as I watched them talk. But perhaps she'd make more money, and I didn't care really. It didn't matter what happened here, only that Sucre finish his road and take us out. It didn't matter what Berman or Sucre or Pedrarias did or did not do, what any of them intended to do. Berman pointed at me. The woman laughed and waved her hand toward the hill: to the new road, to the cemetery, to Jesse and Sucre. It started to rain. She shifted the child to her other arm and they both went inside the shack. The rain was cleaning the red off the steps. I tilted my face to the downpour. I'd stay outside till I was soaked, outside in the mud and rain. Rain poured down the roof, shooting the overhang, churning the mud channel. Berman was the man who'd kissed Jesus the other night. I was certain of it. He just looked ordinary in daylight. He was wearing glasses, like a professor. But he wasn't a professor. He was too greedy, lazy, and dangerous, powerful. Government, mining company, drug cartel. Strong enough, probably, to prevent Sucre from completing his road and keep Pedrarias from his new car. And if Sucre didn't take Jesse dancing we'd never get out. Rain drenched me. Rain and fear and fever were the forces holding me together. What I wanted, beside the road through the jungle to be opened up, was deep and unknown and neither in the future not the past, and had to do with Jesse, Jesse Green. She couldn't be measured in terms of flight or addiction, and interrogation had not spoiled her, nor had Sucre. Jesse was pure existence. She rode easy over the dead and didn't hurt the living because she had given herself all away.

It had stopped raining when Berman came out of the shack, though the trees were dripping. He was hatless and stood looking around the clearing. He started toward the house, then stopped. He walked a few paces to the corner of the woman's little shack and, swaying in the sunlight, pissed against the clay wall. His penis was half-hard, curved like a shepherd's crook. When he was done, he re-entered the hut. After a few minutes I heard the thin wail of a baby. The crying went on and on till the last clouds had rolled away and my shirt was almost dry again. When the tension left my body, I went through the house to the back and listened for the bulldozer's engine.

4.

After the worst heat of the afternoon is over and before the evening insects have woken hungry, the fields are still and cattle come out of their shade to seek grass. These are sick-looking cows. They wade through black broken stalks that the salt has killed, past fenced crops, to a wall of corn. Fat green heads of corn. The corn paths lead through tall yellow-green stems. You must step carefully because of poisonous snakes and spiders. This rich atmosphere clothes you, toes to hat. The cows' bony heads bob on the crest of vegetative waves that the rain has sculpted. Small animals, invisible from above, tunnel under the soil, make furrows along the dirt between the stems. Beyond the cornfield is pasture, then a sloping treeless plain, and crossing the plain is like drifting in a warm sea, through silken intermittent fog, not the drizzle of a Vancouver winter. This gentle passing surface rises toward convent ruins and jungle; at your feet pale yellow gives way to green to horizon blue. And if you slowly spin, closing your eyes, you can imagine yourself upside down, floating in space, head full of blood, a pillar between earth and heaven.

I have found human paths everywhere. When I find one I follow it a while, as though I will discover a lost friend where there are no friends. Sucre says it's late in the season. I've been doing this for days, and never tread the same path twice. The farm fields, the cornfield maze, the pasture. I brush seed and hay from my clothes, from my hair, and walk through the fly-thick cattle till I reach, on a small hill, the shade of the convent ruins where the cows like to lie down in the evening. Each tiny room, defined now by no more than crumbling walls, has its own garden of wild flowers growing among the fallen stones. *Sister. Sister. Sister. Sister.* From this place you can see the cemetery, the tops of the village houses, the estate shacks, the manager's house, even the big villa off by itself with its sapphire pool overlooking the bay. You can see the torn earth of the new road winding out of sight to the port. All this belongs to Pedrarias. But not the ocean beyond the mangroves stretched like a glass sheet, dotted with deep-sea traffic. Not the lighthouse on a distant rock flashing in time to my heartbeat. You cannot see — but I feel it — the other ocean, the opposite sea, the wilder one on the other side of the isthmus, the one that when it meets its counterpart is calmed in the locks of the canal.

The nuns here, before the canal, before the wars, barely felt the world lapping at their walls. I kneel in a corner of one of their cells and a black jet flies over, tearing the air. Magda was the last sister and perhaps this was her room. I pray to Magda to tell me what to do. Parrots answer.

When I'm almost back at the house, I remember I've forgotten to frame a question. What did I want? This morning it had seemed clear. After Pit Meadows, Jesse never wanted another plan. A plan's effectiveness, she said, as with any tool, demands participation, discussion, pros and cons, practice, agreement. And what's the use?

"Are you happy?" Sucre jumped from his blistering machine to my side. Something in me leapt, too, engaged with the fire behind his eyes. "Jesse is happy," he said. "See?"

We both watched Jesse slide down into the mud, barefoot, wearing floral cut-offs and a tank top.

"What about you, lazy dog? Do you know why we are so happy?"

I didn't answer, and Sucre laughed. He and Jesse walked together toward the house.

"A man is here," I yelled. "A guy from a university."

Shouts and crashes came from the shack where Berman had spent the afternoon. A man screamed and a woman answered with single words in a low voice. An old woman ran from the adjacent hut, entered the fight briefly, then reappeared with the wrapped baby. She stood in the doorway, rocking the child. Behind her the young mother's husband emerged roaring and Berman scrambled out holding his boots, avoided a kick, blinked at the sun, and wove in our direction.

Sucre looked back at me, eyebrows raised, then turned to Berman. "Who are you?"

Berman looked confused and rumpled. He kicked over a bucket, sat on it, and began to pull on his boots.

"Who are you?" Sucre repeated.

"My name is Berman. This road." Berman shook back his hair and stared. "The road you are building is illegal, Mr Sucre. You will have to stop. We have notified Pedrarias. Call him, he will tell you to suspend work. The defiance of a court order would mean serious trouble for him and for you."

Sucre wrinkled his nose at Berman. "You have a court order?"

"I have a letter from the head of my department."

Sucre winked at Jesse. "My wife will show you every courtesy," he said. "I must thank you to keep away from me."

He thrust a finger in the direction of the jungle. "As for my road — I am tired. I have had a hard day. My wife will see to you. You have already met her brother."

Berman stood, sinking his heels into the boots. A smile played about his lips. "Mr Sucre, this is not your wife."

Sucre ignored him.

"I understand you have a satellite phone," Berman said.

"Tomorrow. You and I may talk tomorrow. Before you leave."

And Sucre's sausage fingers settled round Jesse's neck, gently turning her, and they stepped across the deep ruts toward the house. Just then the husband flew from the shack and leapt onto Berman's back, leapt away into the trees. A knife dangled from Berman's shoulder. For a moment the violence seemed phoney, the knife a gimmick, a toy. The husband had embraced Berman, surely, only lightly touched the front of the white shirt inside his coat lapels. But the knife was real and Berman, stabbed, fell to his knees in the mud. The mother dashed forward from her hut, stopped just short of me and bent almost double, her hands vanishing into the long skirt between her legs. When I reached Berman, blood was quickly soaking the soft beige padded shoulder of his jacket.

The middle of the night is completely silent. The utter stillness of two oceans and an arching sky. Silence that descends from stars meets in us a frightened silence. Five million years ago the land bridge wasn't even here.

The night sky that seemed, when I first saw it through those windows and that door, like a stage backdrop — such cool stars! — seemed real now.

We were jammed into Sucre's big hammock. I couldn't get out even if I wanted to. We were trapped in Panama, trapped on this estate, trapped in Sucre's hammock. Berman was groaning in my bunk at the back of the house. The village medicine woman had cleaned and dressed his wound after removing the knife and picking rust from deep inside. Now he slept face up, pale, in my bunk.

The tide was high, nearly at the house poles; I could hear it churning. Jesse was asleep against my side. Sucre was soundlessly asleep half on top of her. His weight pinned both of us. I knew it was almost exactly between yesterday and tomorrow. After the weeping and discussion that had gone on late into the night, the shacks were quiet at last, the estate and village as peaceful as those spilled bones alongside Sucre's road.

"You didn't ask your question, now it's too late." Less words than a curdling of the silence. Not unexpected, yet I was wrong about him being asleep. "Are you homesick, little dog?"

"Not with Jesse here," I whispered back.

"Good," he said. "Her tits are getting plumper. She thrives on rice and mussels and beans. She eats up this place." He chuckled. "Pedrarias has a shipping container filled with clothes for her. It's with the car. You should know something. You should know. You should accept that the past is finished with you."

"*Te rogamos . . . Nos permitimos . . .* " Berman's voice a hollow moan in the dark room, dreaming, delirious. "*Santisima Virgen Maria. ¡Para tu hijo!*"

"Do you hate me?" asked Sucre, his hands digging. "If I were you I would hate me." He pushed Jesse against me, her limbs and body pliant. "Do you want to know something else? I will tell you. You will never have revenge on those who have used you."

"Jesse has never used anyone."

"Women grow into their use and their using. Go on. Do what you want. They learn to want what men take. They learn." He bulldozed her body, now conscious, at me. "Can you not do what you want? I think you are a sissy."

"We trust each other. Jesse and me. We look after each other."

"I think she looks after you."

"*¡Dios! Para el Mundo Immaculado . . . Concepsión sin fin, pequeño eje . . . Santisima Virgen Maria . . .* " Berman's voice now was pitched high, each syllable separate.

"Fuck her." Sucre reached between Jesse's legs, cupped his hand under my balls. I shut my eyes. He pulled my cock forward. "Sissy boy. Do it. We are happy because the road is nearly finished. We will drive to the old port, you and Jesse and me."

My cock slithered in his hand, against Jesse. Sucre began to grunt. "Put it inside. It doesn't matter. The future will finish with all of us."

"*Te rogamos . . . Nos permitimos . . .* "

Jesse got up before dawn. I watched her bend over the cot, raise a ladle of water from the pail on the floor to Berman's lips. When next I woke it was light and I was alone in the big hammock. The medicine woman was on the veranda, talking in a low voice to Sucre. He raised his hand impatiently and she squeaked. Coffee was bubbling on the stove, the smell of it sharp in my nostrils. Jesse padded naked across the room toward the door. Berman's face, bathed in sweat, turned; his eyes, wide and clear, watched her pull the old dress over her head.

"Who are you?" he asked.

"Jesse Green," she said. "How do you feel?"

"Get me the phone. Please."

Sucre's feet thumped across the veranda and down the steps. The woman brought in a bowl of hot water in which floated large bright green leaves. Jesse peeled off the shoulder dressing, dipped a cloth in the bowl and wrung it out. First sun struck the mangrove pools. The shoulder was bruised blue. The woman applied the leaves in an elaborate design on top of the wound. The red cloth splashed in and out of the red bowl. I listened to Jesse and the women talking as I pissed behind the flimsy wall at the back of the house, and understood that the husband had beaten and forgiven his wife and gone off to his uncle's village. There was a black widow in the top corner of the back door. Sucre's earthmover grumbled into life.

"Will he die?" I asked Jesse.

"Not today," she said. "Apparently, tonight he will be close. He might die."

Jesse made tea and we sat on the veranda and watched the village women on their way to the mussel grounds. Sucre's machine vanished over the hill in a cloud of smoke.

"Why didn't you go with him?"

"He's pissed off. He didn't want me."

"So everything has changed."

"Yes."

"Berman changes things how?"

"Sucre's nervous. He'll push the road through fast now. Did Berman tell you anything?"

"He says burial sites have been discovered, very old ones. Not from the cemetery. He has found urns." I got the satchel.

Jesse turned the ceramic cover in her hands. "You didn't do what Sucre wanted," she said. "Last night."

"He can't control us."

"No. But he has to think he can." She stood up and stretched her arms above her head. "Yeah," she said. "The ship with the car has arrived. Pedrarias will be at the port in a couple of days."

The laughter of playing children flowed in waves from the village through the compound. Dogs barked in the distance.

"I'm supposed to stay here. Give him water. Clean the wound. Keep him cool."

They were gone. All gone. Jesse left anyway and Berman was asleep or in a coma, so also gone. My face in the bit of mirror nailed to a post on the veranda told me nothing. In my old life I'd been the only familiar thing in an ocean of strangeness till I met Jesse who said she knew me as well as she knew what she looked like every second she was awake. A girl laughing in the cool meadows of my dad's rented-out farm, drop-dead beautiful in faded jeans and halter-top, loose black hair caught with bits of straw. Sunlit, she worked alongside the men, as hard as they worked, and they took side looks at her supple body and her eyes flashed till sunset, and then yard lights, barn lights, dim lights inside the farmhouse brought out my fox caution. In the kitchen Mom and my sister kept vigil while we lay together in the dusty barn. When the farm was all mist, shadows and breathing cows, Jesse'd bare her teeth and tell me about the men who got her wasted and what they'd done to her. Each one a piece of shit, and okay, okay, and that way, and this way, and that's how everything for us had fallen into a kind of shape. We said there was nothing in the universe but us. We didn't need sex, and we would crow-fly to the equator. And now we were stuck at Estancia Pedrarias, empty. Sucre had his road, Berman his life, these women their village and children, Pedrarias his empire. Just for now. But Jesse was transforming. I was a homesick fox. Jesse said we can't have children because we're still kids and kids can't have children. It was pissing rain. Tides swept in and out. Noise, silence. A confusion of colours, then darkness. I had thought the well water smelled like blood until the husband stabbed Berman and I got blood on my hands. Berman was more potent than water. He was like the men at home, and other men we'd met, vain and sly; yet he might have something special for us. Men, Jesse said, were vicious, therefore useful. What they want is in the earth, under the dirt, and they poke at the surface, shove it around, fuck it up. They make holes and tunnels, and you can sneak in and learn something and then crawl out when they're busy filling their pockets. Jesse was the fledgling dragon on the whistle. The mangrove teeming with life, too wild, useless unless filled in. Maybe it was that simple. We just wanted to change, all of us, change into light, and it was time. Sucre said the convent sisters had been forgotten by God. Maybe they transcended. Jesse said we can all transcend if we let ourselves be. If we let ourselves be.

After noon Sucre and Jesse returned. His eyes were glassy, and Jesse chattered like a bird. The road, they said, was rough, but complete and drivable, and tomorrow we'd leave for the docks to claim the car that's been waiting for a week. We'd get to the car before Pedrarias landed at the airport on his private plane.

Berman suddenly sat up. "Send the chopper, please send for it now." Pale and crazy-eyed, he spat and crashed his teeth together. A boy outside was shouting: "New York City has been bombed!"

Sucre went out to talk to the boy. Jesse removed the dry cloth from Berman's forehead, rinsed it in cold water, wiped the sweat from his face and arms and chest.

Berman said, "Call for the helicopter, I beg you," and stared at her as she wet the cloth again, wrung it out, replaced it.

"Ah, professor, you will not be able to sell your pots now," Sucre said from the doorway. "This is the end of America, the beginning of freedom. We must party!" He slapped my back. "Lazy dog!" His arm dangling round my neck. "Americans are kids. They act and dress like kids. Surgeons make America look like a girl. That's why everyone wants to fuck her. Jesus, bring wine!" He counted on his fingers who he had bribed: harbour police, customs, air traffic controllers, the ship's captain, longshoremen. "Now I will take the car for myself," he shouted. "And you know, Jesse, those clothes he bought for you? You will wear them for me. I will take you home, Jesse. And sissy-boy, I will take you home. We will all drive into the apocalypse."

5.

In the night the young mother had gathered her belongings and child, Jesus told us at breakfast, and she'd walked with half the women of the village all the way to her husband's village. Sucre, furious at this unauthorised use of his road, started drinking. He had been chugging beer on the veranda for an hour when Berman got up.

"So professor, you stay with the living!"

Berman sat on the top step of the veranda, very pale, his arm held stiffly to his side. "I will pay you to drive me to the hospital," he said, without turning.

Sucre lit a cheroot, blew smoke at the sun. "I would take you to the hospital, but I have no car, professor."

"You have a bulldozer."

"You owe us the favour of enjoying the life we have saved and not making demands."

"You should ask how much I would pay you."

"You should shut up and listen. Everything is changed today. Let me tell you. Do you know what happened when you were dreaming? Something big."

"What do you mean?"

"Ah, now. Shall we tell him, Ken?"

Jesse came out with a bowl and perched beside him and offered rice on her spoon.

He ignored her. "I can get my hands on a lot of money."

"Are you stupid? You will die before you can pay me back. New York is gone. America is fucked."

"What do you mean?"

"New York is gone. The banks, Wall Street, disco dancing, tall hotels. I built the fucking road and I will use it once. The magic is to use things once, my friend. My road is cleared to the port. We will get Pedrarias's car and drive north and scavenge through the ruins."

"That's fine. Just get me to the port."

Sucre shrugged. "It's out of my hands, professor. I'm not the one to bait, not any more. Try Pedrarias. He is a powerful man. Speak to him."

"Bring me the phone."

"Perhaps," Sucre said.

"What if Mr Pedrarias picks up the car before we get there?" Jesse said.

Sucre set his empty bottle on the deck. "I took you in, didn't I? Even this lazy dog. I built the road. Don't forget." He plucked the cigar from his lips, waved at the huts and trees, ocean and hills. "I was born here. This is my land. You are small people because you were born in a feeble land. You are small. You mean nothing."

He got up and stamped down the steps and went around back to piss. Berman sprawled against the wall, eyes closed. I looked at Jesse. I couldn't take my eyes off Jesse. Light was splashing off her. She looked excited. Her eyes were glittering.

When Sucre returned he took another beer from the cooler, drank from the bottle. He kicked Berman's leg. "Was she worth being stabbed for, professor?"

Berman opened his eyes and nodded slowly. Each sighed heavily. I had the feeling that Jesse and I were watching a movie, and that if one bad guy were to vanish it would destroy the other. It made me feel spaced, dizzy. Except for beer, I was empty, had no weight, so required no support. It didn't matter that I didn't know what I was and didn't know what these men were, because they didn't have a clue either, and they didn't even know they didn't know. They swaggered, heavy with their lives, but right then they seemed quaint creatures, tender as snails.

"She was simple," said Berman, looking up, sly. "Simple."

"These peasants feel much." Sucre dug his fingers into Berman's good shoulder. "Was she as good as the wound is bad?"

Berman flinched.

"Look at this one." Sucre pointed his thumb at Jesse. "You stay here and rot and she is turned on."

He started to laugh. He laughed and laughed, then Berman joined in. They were both laughing. Skeletal cows appeared on the crest of the hill, brown heads above the corn pointing this way and that. Berman groaned and cupped his sore shoulder.

"It's better to feel," Jesse said.

The men laughed harder. The cattle reminded me of the funeral urn — a living rim design on the horizon. Sucre got another two beers from the cooler, perched on the edge of his chair to open them. "Come on, drink, professor. If I tell you women are the second thing on every man's mind, you'll know the first thing is money, and working for it keeps you busy till you've used yourself up and you're so tired you can't even think about women. You were careless, but at least you are alive to tell the tale. So say to me," he said, "how much can you promise me?"

6.

I didn't learn the names of the trees. I didn't learn the flowers or the birds. I didn't learn the use of anything or the meaning of anything. I knew that this wasn't Pit Meadows, didn't need flowers or birds or trees to tell me that. Quick as a fox in only one way, I knew nothing except Jesse. She could topple towers in New York. She could mean anything, make anything happen. Next morning Sucre herded us like sheep into the glassed-in cab of his machine, crowded with screens and buttons. Berman lay propped up against our packs behind Sucre's chair. He was awake at first, then, as we got going, climbing and falling like a cockroach across a bombed field, the blood quit his face and he went lily white, dozing, his head drooping forward as if he was curious about something, trying to make out a detail in an invisible book or map. Sucre, after all his talking, was quiet, his fingers tight on the controls, staring straight ahead. Jesse rode between his knees and I stood beside his armrest.

We bounced onto the rough road, the sun rising behind us out of the black sea. Jesse nudged my toe and we turned to watch the convent ruins till they were blurred by dust. His road was little more than a rutted track, with uprooted trees in piles to either side, their roots clinging to soil, still moist. At the cemetery a great tangle of vines smouldered. It must have been near there that the older graves and the bones and shards had been found, but Berman was too groggy to ask. And then the road turned away and we were passing cane fields and cornfields where I recognised some of the people working. I remembered driving Dad's car a hundred-sixty klicks an hour along the Alberta highway, watching the needle climb. I remembered when I was a kid riding in the back of a truck to Alouette Lake for a family picnic, giggling as the car skidded sideways when another car came at us. All those times driving my drunken father from the bar to the farm. That awesome ride home from the bank with Jesse the day we got going, quit drugs, took a powder, booked out of there, split, got loose, hit the road.

When Sucre saw three women walking, he slowed down and shouted, "Nice, eh, hermosas? Make your life easier, no? You will go like this right to the city."

From then on, it was all jungle. Whenever we passed someone, Sucre called out: "What a convenience, isn't the road great?"

Cradled against Sucre's fat armrest, rocked by the rutted track, I got drowsy and let my head fall in a kind of half-sleep.

"Wake up, Ken," he called. "You will dance with me tonight, yes?"

"Leave him alone," said Jesse.

"I don't know why," he said. He tweaked the collar of Jesse's dress, then replaced his fingers on the controls. "I feel sad today."

"Think of the car," she said. "You will soon be driving the car."

"I know. I know."

The road was terrible. Sucre was cursing, and I realised that his project was not finished, he had abandoned the job — perhaps because of Berman, or Pedrarias, or the

Towers, or the whole cocktail, but we had to crawl along, among half-buried tree trunks and strewn branches, over great mud hills, avoiding crevasses. There was no way a car, even a four-wheel drive, could use this road.

Jesse slipped around Sucre's chair to check on Berman. "He's very hot," she said.

I turned. The professor was out of it and his bandage completely red.

"The town is not far," said Sucre.

The bay looked empty until through the trees we saw hundreds of tiny boats with dirty sails on the blue-green water, and then we were blinded, on the loose gravel of a little street of adobe huts on one side and low brick buildings on the other. The huts gave way to houses and office buildings. The port was a jumble of corrugated shacks and warehouses and cement-block buildings crowded into the narrow foreshore, half taken up with hotels and skyscrapers. Sucre parked in front of a bank's double glass doors.

"You bring back the money, Mr Berman, and I'll get you to the hospital."

Berman didn't move.

Two security guys wearing revolvers were walking toward us.

"To hell with you," Sucre said and got the bulldozer rolling again.

At the hospital Sucre and I lifted Berman down and laid him on the blacktop by the doors. A nurse rushed out waving a clipboard. "What has happened to this man? You must fill in papers!"

Sucre shrugged. I gave her Berman's leather satchel. Orderlies appeared with a gurney as we pulled out of the parking lot.

We abandoned the bulldozer at the gate to the docks. I felt sick again, really sick. The air smelled of fruit, rancid coconut, seaweed, sulphur. Generators droned on, loud as a city. *Nausea* was a book Jesse and I read. "To love someone you have to jump across an abyss. My place is nowhere. I am unwanted." I puked beside a corrugated shed, exquisitely red in the late sun, Sucre peering through a paint-spattered window, rapping his knuckles on the glass. I grazed my palm along the wall and it came away powdered with rust. A skinny man in a dark suit and white sneakers opened the door and led us along narrow alleys between tall warehouses, across little courtyards. Somewhere near here the cops had grabbed us. We passed a bar, the stink of beer and cigars horrible, and came to a ship moored to iron cleats by thick cables, the hull reaching into the sky, the four of us stopped in deep shadow. I was blown away. Another book we read was *On the Road*. "A pain stabbed my heart, as it did every time I saw a girl I loved who was going the opposite direction in this too-big world."

Across from the ship was a warehouse with doors you could drive a crane through right next to a regular-sized door.

"She is in here," said the skinny guy. I could smell him, his sweat and breath, sweet with rum.

"Here!" Sucre thrust out an envelope and the guy took it delicately.

The darkness inside the warehouse was hot, fat and slimy. Light can't penetrate such air, and I couldn't see Sucre, couldn't see Jesse, though they were right in front of me, breathing. Then a bank of overhead floods rained light so pure it woke up silver wheel rims and bolts and handles.

"A beauty," the skinny guy said. "A sexy Latin beauty." He leaned toward Jesse, then rolled his eyes at Sucre. "It's World War Three now."

The car was hunched in the centre of the cement floor, a glossy black pool that a fish might break from. When Sucre got to it he stroked the sleek scientific curve, dipped his hand, broke the surface.

A battered wood case, padlocked and bound with scarred leather straps, stood by the car.

"Let's see inside," said Sucre.

"Be quick," said the skinny guy. He tossed the keys.

Sucre unlocked the case and opened it. He crooked a finger at Jesse. "Try something on."

"Here?" said Jesse.

"Go ahead," said Sucre. He folded his arms. "Take a look. See if you like anything."

The skinny guy was going to protest, then just put his hands in his jacket pockets when Jesse sank her arms in and the colours danced and riffed. It was theatre. The men looked like patient proud dads. We were human audience. We were bears. We were gorillas. Jesse picked through soft leather boots, silk hats, sundresses, jackets, a klatch of skirts, swimsuits, underwear, tossing a selection on the hood of the car where they floated, slipped, mixed, and finally she set a small glass box of jewellery on the stained cement floor.

Sucre and the skinny guy laughed as Jesse pulled her old dress off over her head and stuffed it inside the trunk, her body a matter of fact, the physical girl, but also substance and essence inside out. These men were growing unsure of something. Control, yes, but something else. I couldn't lift a finger, could only witness. Oil collected on my lips.

"All of this counts," she said, her body blazing. "It's part of our ticket."

The world beyond the doors, gulls screaming and a longshoreman singing, was fathoms beneath this brilliant heaven, blinding white, as she dressed, paying critical note to every wrinkle in the black tights, fine fishnet, snapping the elastic against her belly. "What d'you think?"

"Of course," said Sucre.

"*Maria*," whispered the skinny guy.

"Now this," she said. Black silk shirt and a short pleated black skirt. Soft flat-soled ankle-high black leather boots. Wide leather-and-chain belt, leather-and-chain necklace, big silver earrings.

"Okay?"

"Okay."

"Okay. Okay?"

"Hot."

"A rich little orphan."

She stepped forward and put sunglasses over my eyes then shrugged into a thin dark leather aviator jacket, folding the black fleece collar evenly down in front and behind, then tugged on a black leather cap and black leather gloves, and posed directly under one of the floods, feet apart, gloved fingers stretched to the ceiling, and her shirt rode to her ribcage, her belly-button ring flashed.

The myth looks like the sand map, before any cities, of a prehistoric swamp. The modern bear and gorilla shift foot to foot as Jesse twirls once, the skirt fanning out, and then sits on the case, her legs wide, chin on one hand.

"Let's go," said Sucre. "Show's over." He turned his back on her, slid into the driver's seat and the car purred into life. He revved the motor. Rolled down the window. Popped the hood.

The skinny guy, an automaton now, lifted the case in. The trunk was the hood. He pointed a remote control at an electrical panel on the wall; one of the great doors swung open to warm salt air, ship's lights, thousand-foot cranes and wheeling gulls, a line of arc lamps on poles.

We were on a lonely street late at night, the car nearly soundproof, almost silent. A girl's leather jacket squeaked against a leather seat. A man's breath, thick with frustration. The dash patterned with electric blue, green, red numbers and symbols, the armrest bristling with silver switches. There was Sucre's sunburned neck, Jesse's black-nest hair. My hand smelled of rust and sweat. I wanted no one to speak. Not Jesse, not Sucre. What was important was that no one should try to describe the feeling inside the warehouse when we had all been aware of something.

7.

Jesus was being interviewed on the hotel-room TV about the attempted murder and subsequent kidnapping of Professor Berman, then the news anchor's voice said the police were seeking Miguel Sucre in connection with recent violence at the Estate Pedrarias. "Paul Berman, a professor and businessman in the mining industry has been admitted to the Central Hospital with life-threatening injuries." A photograph of Berman appeared on the screen.

"Tonight you dance with all men," said Sucre. "You will dance with whoever I say. I am going out for a while."

From our room we had a view of the town, the harbour, ships at dock, three at anchor in the bay. The million lights were hard to take after only lamplight, faint glimmers from the village shacks, for weeks. Traffic noise rose to the window mixed with coarse voices and exhaust fumes, and something in me started to buzz, like a long hit of skunk over crack.

I sat crosslegged on the bathroom floor watching Jesse soak in the tub. "Why don't we leave now?"

"We could, but we'd get nothing."

"What can we get?"

A rooster crowed down in the street, very near, then a dog began to bark and she stood, water beading on her skin.

"Something's changed. Like a huge change." She shook her head fast and her hair whipped out, cool spray. "Can you feel it?"

"I can feel it," I said. "Yeah."

In the room were two double beds, and I curled up on one while Jesse laid out clothes on the other. White shorts and a red halter-top, blue jeans and steel T-shirt, cream lace camisole and jodhpurs . . . I dozed, eyes half shut while she counted, matched, tried on, compared, discarded, talking to herself.

"Eleven costumes, eleven gates. The black outfit is the first gate." She wiggled back into her warehouse skirt, arms wide to her reflection in the full-length mirror. Black hair against jet-black shirt, red neon highlights. "Eleven different girls."

"Eleven?" I asked.

"If you dance with me, then I won't mind anything. It will work out."

I sat on the edge of the bed. "Is this what we planned in Pit Meadows?"

She cocked her head. She played with her hair, lips pursed. She turned from the mirror and laid her hands on my shoulders. "We are okay. We're together and we're not hiding anything from each other, right?"

"Sucre isn't really powerful," I said.

"It's beginning," she said.

Then Sucre was in the room, lifting Jesse to her feet, grabbing her ass, bunching the black skirt. "You are a sexy little ghost, cuchura. So pale." He pulled away and tossed me a white plastic bag. "This is so you can come, too." In the bathroom he splashed water on his face, spread suds over his beard, and shaved.

Inside the bag was a white suit. I put it on. I looked handsome, older. I went out onto the balcony and closed my eyes and saw a body stretched on a rocky beach. A dead girl, blue and shiny, striped with wet seaweed. A dead boy, blue and shiny, striped with wet seaweed. Gold is still passing through this land, kissing men's fingers. Jesse's clothes from America, Europe, Japan, a thousand skirts on a thousand girls, tell little stories in a million heads — such a skirt, such legs, the end always the same symptom, the small useless invention to mask the lie. Ghosts are greedy and we pay the price in beauty by waiting and waiting for them to decide to haunt. Every time gold passes hands traders are devalued. We must look for the bliss between people, not the transaction, that's what Jesse told me. We must look for the signs of stress — starvation, obesity, sorrow — and we must leap the abyss into each other's arms before the crack is too wide.

Sucre washed soap from his cheeks, cleaned his ears with the corner of a towel, put on a new shirt, tan trousers, a light linen jacket.

I helped Jesse pack the ten outfits. Sucre called for a porter and while we waited he shared his bottle with me, ignoring her. The porter carried the case to the elevator and we all rode to the lobby where, in the mirrored walls, I spied three strangers, a fat father and two children, a child in black, one in white, lost in a forest of potted trees.

8.

The air on high, cool in the car, one road into another following the bay's steep hills, coasting from jungle to the beach, blowing by buildings around the harbour.

·   Each bar was just another drinking hole and more or less the same as any bar anywhere despite Jesse's changes, each response to her display duplicating the ones before in nearly every detail. Sucre would have the first dance, then every guy he wanted got to dance with Jesse, and there were a lot — not because she was more beautiful and younger and better dressed than the other girls, but because Sucre was working his large angle. Some of her partners were brilliant forest birds, some terrible raptors. Their shrieks got louder as the night got busier and more complex, and I didn't know the dialect, didn't know how to say words, not in any language, but they danced away, danced, and across the globe were wars and conflagration and mass exodus while here something warm, tender, got released into the air (small love, solitaire, burdened by habit), then something tart, risky. Sucre ebbed and flowed. One minute he was at my side, watching Jesse Green, next he was in deep conversation with some guy, next I saw him through the window at the curb, leaning on his car, showing kids the dash lights and stick shift and glove box. The four leather bucket seats. Sometimes he treated them to a ride round the block. Between clubs he parked on dark streets and Jesse picked her next clothes and scrambled into them by the light from the open trunk while he pissed in an alley.

On a narrow lane in a thunderous industrial zone, where the air vibrated heavy monotonous shit from a nearby factory, Jesse Green took off her black outfit and pulled on red tights and high red boots and got into a red slick mini-dress, zippered crotch to throat, and I helped her with the pink earrings, and clipped twelve gold bangles on her right wrist.

Next, she stood on a wide sidewalk between the car and a brick building with rows of high, dark windows, and unzipped the red dress, peeled the boots and tights and put on cream cotton panties, cream socks, tight faded yellow jeans, tan suede shoes, and there were angry words from above, and light spilling from windows. The shirt was pale gold silk and ended above her navel, the long sleeves embroidered with yellow thread, and when I looked up, men were hanging out the windows, watching her tits push out pure gold, so I buttoned her shirt up tight, and saw the shadow on her belly, that gully that splits a person right from left.

Sucre rode more kids round the block. Jesse and I waited on the sidewalk between tall office buildings. On the other side of the street was the bank we'd tried earlier in the day. The road was under construction. Fences of rough wood barricaded a long trench that disappeared into the distance, marked by flashing orange lights. When Sucre roared back and parked, he and I sat on the front of the car and with the slouching kids watched Jesse take off her clothes.

She shrugged away the shirt, kicked off shoes and socks, slid down jeans and panties (skin pale as paper in the orange flashes) and put on a sky-blue lace bra, slipped into a blue lycra bodysuit, pushed her feet into blue boots with spike heels, and the kids lost interest and wandered off.

Sucre offered me a cigar and a blue flame.

Jesse angled a navy beret on the side of her head, crouching beside the car to study herself in the passenger window. Round her neck she clipped an azure pendant, *yoni*, and in her ears midnight earrings, *lingam*. Short asymmetrical royal-blue leather wrap skirt, long buttonless alpaca coat thrown over her right shoulder.

The next place we parked was near the docks and I could smell the sea and something dead that gulls were fighting over near an old motorcycle partly hidden behind overflowing trashcans.

Sucre wound up the windows. "Okay, Jesse. Ken, get into the front with me."

"Why?"

We sat gazing out of the windshield of the air-conditioned car.

In the headlights she undressed and stood naked a moment looking at the motorcycle, then up at the stars, her body slick with sweat from the hours of dancing, then she put on a short belted olive-green trench dress and cyan high heels.

"She's a good girl," he said. "You're both good kids."

"It's so hot," she said, getting into the back of the car. "Am I glad to get rid of the alpaca."

My jaw ached from clenching so much, and my teeth were coated with the dark oil that kept backing up from my stomach. We stopped at a gas station to buy toothbrushes. In the washroom I cleaned my teeth and watched myself in the mirror. Qué sopá? The floor was wet and muddy. I sat on the toilet and massaged my scalp, my forehead, with cool wet fingers. Back at the car Sucre was gone. I put my feet on the dash and wiggled my toes in the air from the vent.

Jesse peeped over from the back seat. "You look sick."

"I feel sick. Where's Sucre?"

She shrugged. "Setting something up. Some kind of business."

"You okay?"

"Yeah. But I'm about done. How far are we?"

"You said eleven gates."

"Yeah."

"Half way. We could steal the car."

"I've thought about it."

"We could take off right here, right now."

"We've got no money, no papers."

"We'd have the car."

"Stolen car." She yawned. "We have to finish now."

"What's he up to?" I said.

"Same as always. He's going down."

I turned up the air, aimed all the vents, leaned back and closed my eyes.

In the alley behind the next club, Jesse unfastened the belt and the trench dress fell open in trunk light and she pulled on a lavender T-shirt, stepped into a fringed amethyst jean mini-skirt, held up a linen jacket as if it weighed nothing.

"What d'you call that colour?" Sucre asked me.

"Kind of pink," I said. "Fuchsia."

"Fuchsia?" he said.

"Yes. Pale fuchsia. Definitely."

Sucre shook his head. Jesse hooked the jacket on her shoulders then pulled on lilac leather gloves and popped her feet into violet slip-ons.

At the seventh gate we were nearly at the end of the night and a lot of kids Sucre had been showing off his car to were running behind, and when they began to anticipate our route and took short cuts Sucre laughed and tried to outfox them with speedy turns in low gear, swearing at them through his open window, urging them on, swerving left and right, and each time they fell behind, he'd turn a corner and they'd appear from an alley ahead, fewer in number, a smaller and smaller gang of girls and boys, maybe ten to fifteen years of age.

We parked in front of an old building with a clock tower, and the kids gathered round us, breathless and grinning, and we opened the car doors, blasting them with a radio station playing calypso, and they started to dance round the car. An old woman sweeping the steps of the building leaned on her broom while Jesse danced with the kids, flinging the fuchsia jacket to the oldest boy and the shoes and the skirt to the girls, tossing the T-shirt to another boy. She put on satin tap pants, silver belt, snakeskin trench coat with wide sleeves and deep lapels, satin-bowed low-heeled suede boots, big pearl earrings and a bracelet, and I joined her and we threw bits of costume to the other kids, who calypsoed up and down the steps, and we were all yelling, crazy as shipwrecked slaves, while the sweeper stared and Sucre made a phone call.

"I was diverted," said Sucre. "The night is going well."

"Aren't you tired?" I asked.

He shook his head. "It will be dawn before long. At the next club, I will get you something, both of you, to help you stay awake and have fun. The last place you danced not so good, Jesse."

"It doesn't matter, right, as long as everyone sees me," she said. "That's the point, right? That's what's important?"

"For people to see you?" he said. He laughed. "You think you're your own little legend?"

We came to a wide round tank surrounded by scaffolding. Across from the tank, at a lighted entrance, a group of men were smoking, and when we got out of the car and Jesse pulled her bag from the trunk, they began muttering.

Jesse and I ducked under the scaffolding where water dripped from iron braces above our heads into a mess of dark weeds and there was a smell of rust and brackish water. It was cold in the shadows beneath the metal stairs that spiralled round the tower and Jesse was shivering as she stripped off jewellery, boots, trench coat then pinched the elastic waist of the tap pants. Over at the club entrance the men were peering toward us and Sucre went over to tell them the next bit of his story. Jesse left on the pants and just pulled on a see-through beaded dress with spaghetti straps, crimson shoes. "Okay. Let's go."

"How many gates now?" I said.

"I thought you were counting."

"I've lost track."

In the bar there was no dancing at all, just a little stage and two men taking forever to remove their clothes, while other dopey men watched, heads nodding slower and slower, and even the musician seemed to doze, mouth open, over his beat-up guitar. Sucre nursed a drink, this time with no business to occupy him, and seemed dull and depressed. He took off his dark glasses, rubbed his eyes. The place was so sleepy and dark that it took a long time for anyone to notice us. When they did, Jesse took to the stage and there was sparse clapping and a guy put his lips to my ear and said, "You do it, boy."

I shook my head. I couldn't do it. I thought I couldn't. But I could.

I got up there beside Jesse and the applause got louder and we took off our clothes and grabbed each other and held on for a long time. We were anonymous, androgynous. When the catcalls started, I snatched up our clothes and took her hand and we ran from the bar. Under the water tower I put on my white suit again. Under the water tower Jesse flicked off her spaghetti straps, zipped down and peeled off her dress and panties. Her beads clattered on the scarred boards.

"Go get him," she whispered. "Tell him we're ready to go."

Everyone had fallen asleep. Sucre was nodding at the table. Maybe his mouth was a little sadder. Maybe the guitarist had actually passed out — the strings he held with his left hand were as still as his right hand. As I crossed the room, a guy said, "You better leave. Look what you have done."

There was hardly a person on the street now, just the shuffling homeless, no kids, no other cars, and this time Jesse wore flesh-coloured panties, French-cut, tight thigh-high boots with wide tops, pale leather, an infrared lycra mini-dress, and the next club was rich and there was no sign of other girls or women. Two old men in floral shirts came right over to Jesse and put their fingers down the wide tops of her boots.

Sucre was very pleased. "These guys are members of our government," he said. "They are very powerful. You should lose yourself completely."

They peeled bills from large rolls, flapped the money in Sucre's face, pushed their moustaches against Jesse's face and their fingers on the infrared dress, calling pals over to feel the puss-in-boots, this hot chikita was an oven, feel, feel, man, feel, till I couldn't see her, just a flash of red muscle, her voice telling them where to go, getting them worked up and letting them in where they wanted as long as clothes stayed in place, calf-skin boots, yes, slick as a fish, don't worry, baby, lycra stretches, it stretches easy, see, see? Sucre over in a corner of the room arguing with a man wearing a huge diamond ring.

There was no one on the street now, and all the clubs were closed. Sucre said we should quit, but Jesse said one more, there must be one more, and he said he knew a place that stayed open forever. She wiped off her body with the red dress under the flashing arrows of a movie marquee across from a taxi stand where the driver of the only cab was smiling in his sleep, his head on a fringed cushion propped against the open window, bare feet sticking out the opposite window. An old poster behind the cashier's chair in the ticket booth showed a rich woman sitting on a bed across from a mirror in a room full of antiques. *Last Year with Delphine.* In the booth glass my face looked stunned and green and Jesse's movements were unnaturally snappy.

Sucre's smile, as she stepped out wearing a transparent bodysuit, ultraviolet silk gym shorts, three chain-and-leather belts, a handful of pearl ropes, and purple running shoes, looked guilty, pained.

"I feel like an old man who has seen and done everything, good and bad," Sucre said. We were driving along the coast, out of the town. The sky showed just a little light. "I feel like I am going to my execution. I liked everything. I liked my life, even the difficult things, but all my plans come to an end now."

"Stop here," said Jesse. "I need to pee."

She leapt from the car and I was right behind her through the archway entrance into a park and as soon as we were inside the land felt spacious, nothing forever but a faint path in dead grass to a statue of a man holding a rifle by a dead fountain from which no water flowed, and a stone bench in front of weedy flower gardens and little bare hedges. Jesse tossed me her last costume, a pure white dress that, crushed, fit into my fist. It felt good to walk in a garden, however dead. Small birds were waking up. The sky was brightening. Jesse ditched the belts and jewellery, tore off the shorts and bodysuit, and left them on the bench. She pulled on a white cap and sauntered out onto the dry lawn. The stars up there were pale. I draped the white dress over the back of the bench and lay down,

just for a second, and immediately saw a shooting star. Then
a satellite. Another satellite. Another shooting star. When I
opened my eyes a bright veil covered the sky and treetops and
delicious cool air was rising from the ground. I rolled onto my
side and there was Jesse barefoot in the middle of the brown
grass in shimmering white.

When I woke again there were people in the park,
gardeners, children, young couples with infants. The dress
lay dead under the bench. I couldn't remember what had
happened, where Jesse had gone. I got to my feet and down on
the grass was the white velvet cap embroidered with rose vine.
An ugly laugh made me look round. One of the gardeners,
bent nearly double, was squinting at me and cackling. Near
the fountain a grey-haired man in a spotless white suit was
feeding pigeons grain from a paper bag. The earth began to
shake at that moment and water stuttered from the fountain,
dribbled out, then jetted upward. Terror and elation. Pigeons
tore away with a ripping sound to join crows circling the park.
When I looked again, the fountain was sending up spray, its
stone basin was brimming, and the old man had gone.

That was the last time I saw Jesse, Jesse Green in a white
dress with only one sleeve, silver-threaded lace inserts at each
hip, skin behind, the thinnest blue vein. I think it was her, but
really it might have been any girl.

9.

A fresh breeze blew against my face. There was the deafening noise of big machines working somewhere ahead, toward the estate. A white man in army fatigues was sitting in the back of a parked land cruiser yelling into a satellite phone; his driver, Jesus, was not pleased to see me.

"What are you doing here?"

"Have you seen her?"

"Yes I have seen her. Up at the convent. You know, man," he said. "You should leave. Look at all the damage you've caused." He leaned out of the land cruiser. "They caught Sucre. The police are looking for you. You can't stay here."

Beyond a little rise the entire road was red and at intervals along its edges were many broken burial urns, some red but most in black-on-white panels. Thousands of shards. I followed a shore of shell fragments and shards arranged into red waves and kneeled down to tug an urn from the heap. The urn, broken in two equal parts, came together in my hands. Smooth as skin. Perfectly together, yet broken. No lugs or handles. I stopped at a pile of bones and there, right in the middle of the new road, in a soft bed of crushed shells, two skeletons lay parallel to each other about six feet apart.

I felt dizzy with the sun on my back and head and crouched and picked at the layers at the edge of the shell bed. The next urn was complete, and decorated with a raised red double-snake design. Inside was a circle of small crumbling bones.

PEDRARIAS ESTATE SITE - Results of four test pits
  Simple flake points
  Polished stone celts
  Spindle whorls
  Incised spindle whorls

Proof of the presence of the following has been absolutely ascertained:
  Painted urns
  Painted ware
  Red ware vessels
  Polychrome red ware
  Panelled red ware
  Cocle-type red line ware
  Incised relief brown ware
  Brown ware whistles

The quantity of sherds present indicates that further excavation is of paramount importance. Evidence suggests that the following artefacts already restored from sherds found in proximate sites might be restored from sherds recovered from the Pedrarias site:
  Incised monkey urn
  Votive ware double turtle-monkey effigy
  Votive ware double bird effigy
  Lizard effigy vessel
  Humpback effigy jar
  Serpent burial urn

An entire double serpent burial urn has been recovered containing the skeleton of a female child. Two parallel skeletons have been found in a shell lens. Both had the wide-open mouth, and the head in hypertension, with the occiput in contact with the cervical spine, that indicates sacrifice burial. One was a young male, the other female. At the feet of the female was the double serpent urn containing the skeleton of the child.

This Pedrarias Estate double serpent urn has yielded a radiocarbon date of AD 198 plus/minus 80.

Life would have been quiet and nondescript with little conflict, and with almost no contact with other tribes, though occasional dangerous journeys might have been made along the coast. Clay skills were highly developed, but full classic polychromes have not been proved. Weaving was practised. Human sacrifice was practised suggesting a stratified class system. Burial was ritualistic, and the dead were placed in urns, or laid in the ground, open extended. Some mutilation occurred.

10.

Out of the mangroves, uphill, away from the rutted tree-strewn road, past the estate, past the village, to the convent ruins. First night at the jungle's edge, at the base of a huge tree (not ash, not birch, not cedar, not elm, not fir, not maple, not oak, not poplar, not spruce), among polished wood knees and elbows, to dream of Jesse Green. Half awake in the big roots, the stars buzzing, it's too late for me to pick up the trail where we left off. It is all about us, after all, isn't it? Me and Jesse and the land bridge. Dawn brings Magda. I have taken a wrong turn and lost Jesse and found Magda. Her face made of clay shards.

All day in the ruins I've been thinking about my mother, missing her. Then at dusk Magda shows herself again at the edge of the forest under a flock of birds crossing the sun far to the west. I lean forward till the top of my head touches red earth, then carefully kick my feet into the air. Balanced, a pillar between heaven and earth. Along the ground cows hang in the sky. A new moon rises up the hill, and down below, tangled in the mangrove, is the yellow excavator stuck in the swamp since yesterday. The air is extremely clear. The nuns' old stones transmit warmth to my scalp and palms. Cicadas chirp and a small plane flies over the lighthouse rock. Sweat runs from the small of my back to my neck. Miles beyond the rock little islands are visible. Among them, the tiny smudge of an approaching storm turns the water grey.

My sister has a broken back and brain damage. She seems to know our mother, but no one else. They spend weeks on end inside the house travelling room to room. Jesse wanted us free of family, drawbridge politics, us and them, wanted us unjealous and detached, so we could be intimate with the unmade world and with the animals. She wanted to disorient herself. This trip, our *entanglement*, she called it, our leap, was a preparation for something we wanted or somewhere we wanted, but weren't able to see yet. She told me that water was the essential and original element and Panama was the gate between the two great oceans, and we would open it. We only needed time. And then and then. And now and now and now I'm upside down at the centre of a cosmogony, and will do well to begin my part of the task. Magda dances at the edge of the jungle. She is attempting to delay the excavation. Jesse will find me. She made a promise. She said opening the land bridge would open us, and maybe that's what is happening. But there are so many levels, so many tiny separate existences. On my lips — is it water or oil? I don't know. What's swimming and what's been drowned? Jesse will find me. Flamingos are coming. Listen. That's the whiplash of pinions. We'll see them in a minute. The storm is bigger and closer and faster.

There they are. A pink mist.

Countless bright rose-coloured birds trailing long skinny legs.

They fly directly over my extended feet, toward the sinking sun and the canal, ahead of the storm from the east, which has advanced and grown. My legs topple and I sit upright, dizzy, while the flamingos sail over, a clatter of messages and warnings. Now a third of the sky is covered by cloud. I love

Jesse Green and when she comes back she will find me with the Sisters in the Convent or with Magda in the forest. Life will be made of prayers, worship, listening hard for something we've never heard before, working our whole life in silence trying to figure out whether beauty comes from outside or inside. It isn't about power. It isn't about cruelty. The storm bears down on the sea, wind kicking up waves. More flamingos rise from the shore beyond the mangrove and let the wind lift them up and up till they fall sideways and drop landward. When I drop my feet, I'm two years old, shirt pressing against my back, billowing in front, pants ballooning. God grabs me hard by the neck and ankles and I flap like a flag before the hissing rain.

Water is everywhere, my lips taste of salt.

I grasp the whistle like a referee and lie on my back in the slight shelter of a stone wall and cross my hands over my chest, and rain falls, wind keens through cracks in the stones. It will be dark soon. I'm staying here to pray for every person I can remember. The whole hillside whines. Lightning strikes ten feet to my right. Pebbles roll across packed dirt. Water might be everything, but fire will be the end. I love Jesse Green. She is still a child. Rain splashes my face and chest till I pull off my clothes and wash my dusty feet then lie down again to pray for every animal I can remember and all those I can't name and all the ancestors of all those I can and can't name. Ghosts make sudden rushes this way and that, as though armies are passing, regiments passing. My dad's face among the millions, then gone, faster than light. Clouds directly overhead like boulders and water gushes down and the ground turns to mud and the light is nearly gone over the sea faintly blue sun a yellow notch on the horizon boiling clouds the tilting sea my body like ice *get up get away come back* stagger down the slope against the wind this ground is a vessel for the wind this ground is a vessel for the wind I am an organ for the wind kneeling in the mud not safe and not lost sounding the snake whistle and the lighthouse flashes a figure by the house is waving she runs straight toward me up the hill to tell me something about the nuns what they have done slips in the mud rises goes down again I have been struck there's too much pressure in my head from sudden darkness and rain look won't you look at my white knuckles blow the whistle again sun vanishes stars arrive stars and the black east ocean sickle moon again beside my empty hand higher than *nuns remember everyone with love they think only of God the task at hand and one another.*

No One But Himself

1.

The midwife argued with the doctor who hauled him out with forceps anyway, and with a thunderclap he washed up on shore and the line was cut. The lights were so bright. He was abandoned, shipwrecked, a castaway who couldn't stop talking, but for five days the best he could do was a half-dead fly in a swaying web in the white place while other babies who would not listen rolled around and howled.

When the nurse scooped him up and carried him down corridors, he met pirates and tried English, Dutch, French, African dialects, Indian dialects, American tribal dialects, Spanish. The nurse whispered she was a nun from Convent of Las Consebinas and warned him of the unhealthy air of Porto Bello.

Back at his mother's breast he took a nipple in the afternoon, half listening to familiar rumbles from a man who had lost his rights to this dry harbour that tasted of home: "Amorous barbarous collusion, destitute epiphany." He'd never seen such rain. The window was streaming. His mother's breasts were streaming. All was black and white and blue.

The man smiled at him but blankly, and continued to rumble.

All manner of things and animals and people were gathered, waiting, and now would listen just to him. Except the foliage was in the way, as was concern for his mother, as was his own size and ability, as were walls and windows. He needed, among other things, to explain that he was no bird or copycat or urchin. Nobody should have doubts at this age. He turned from the nipple to question the man, but was shipwrecked again on the same hostile sterile promontory. He interrogated a castle owner about his scorched-earth policy. "Up the Chagre River west of Colon into the jungle with a force of twelve hundred."

There were noise-like words and word-like sounds; he played with both but did not have the meaning knack, though he was beginning to grasp and manipulate the flashes when exhaustion hit him like a fleshy wall.

It went on like this, rescue and shipwreck, the nun carting him along riverbeds to his mother, back to the white place (floaty web in the window), to his mother, to the white place and web, to his rumbling father. He shaped his voice till it was full of plaint, a confession if that would do, an apology if that would do the trick, a summation of the events of his life so far, a comparative study of pre- and post-womb societies, attempts that he knew were going nowhere and which he should not expect ever to end. Nothing had prepared him. Each rescue took him past rows of faces and to each he pled his case: should a human soul be so treated? Was this capture and release? Was this the price to pay for an audience? Were they his wide continuous diverse family and he the sole performer? He tried the blue wheel, combustion, shuttle-cock, the reformation, re-priming the pump, binary fission, and was working on knitting when the egg cracked, the wind freshened and blew the roof off, and he was bouncing in his mother's arms away from hospital smells and into new inter-locutions and challenging protocols.

He opened his mouth and spoke to a crow, a street, eight houses and a freighter. He spoke to heat and cold and his father's prickly stinky friends, icicles and sunbeams and uncle's fingers. What did he tell? It was a long unbroken description of all he'd seen before the time of wreckage and rescue, and it was nuanced and detailed, a portrait of God in a cosmic gallery, the flares and iridescent explosions from wars that must be recounted, for this was important, this was the prehistory of his species. The birth of fingernails, the right to choose, the mouthful of scavenged antelope, the loggia with a view, a baseball hat on a battlefield, the *think-am* man, the industrial revolution, the musical *always* of his mother's voice singing on and on except at night, dreams that would open all the doors and windows, and angels lining up for the rickety roller-coaster that was being assembled and would soon take up all the space in the backyard and . . .

Creatures nodded and made trilling noises, but made no sign that they understood what he was telling them.

He kept extolling the epic. They kept interrupting. He grew desperate. It began to fade. Its vivid urgency diminished. And then at last he began to understand the level of their expectations of themselves and of him. At first disheartened with the paltry traffic they taught him to use in glory's place, and then horrified, he talked ferociously, passionately, to everyone.

Then when he was two a woman with a large face and loose throat praised his foot.

"What a little foot," she said. "Such a pretty foot."

He was dumbstruck. He stopped talking in amazement.

She took his foot in her rough hand and held it to her cheek. The heat of her hand, the penetration of her stare.

And he stopped and felt the simple separate pieces that he'd been noticing lately (but needed to ignore because he couldn't connect them) fit together.

The new terrible confusions began with socks, which foot to which sock? which sock to which shoe? and proceeded through buttons and the discovery of size and order — his pants button would fit into his mother's shirt's torn buttonhole but that was wrong — and vehicles, which side? how turn? why was outside inside in transit? He was a vital tiny speck in the thrust of things who had been awarded a voice big enough to infiltrate every nook and mall and empyrean his senses butted up against, and the urge to describe such forays, and he was reduced to geography. He tried to please his mother but it was useless. She found him perfectly flawed. And as far as his dad was concerned he was a show-off.

Then came the period of cuts and stomach-aches and here is the potty (the summit of his tribe's cultural accomplishments), do a Good One.

He spoke to everyone, adapting the plain system he'd inherited, and said nothing of interest, as far as he was concerned, until he was twenty-six and met his cousin Emma in the university cafeteria amid a blinding riot of silver slashing light, crash of crockery, chirping voices. He didn't hear a word she said and none of her communication reached him, except for the way she leaned. The way she leaned, listening to him, shaped something similar, a kind of twirl, in him.

Charles decided that from then on he'd speak as if he belonged to a race of speakers who would only speak to those who knew how to listen. And Emma was the queen of listeners. The twirl turned into a squirm. *Be careful*, he said to himself. *Conserve.*

2.

The girl who listened began with geese. Because she was born in spring their loud arrival heralded hers, but by September all her friends were flying south and she heard for the rest of her life in all voices only endings, farewells. She lay on her back as still as she could and listened to her mother's stories of going away. The Genesis list of *au revoir*; Moses on the lam; Noah and all the animals, the lamb with the key, poor Satan and the end of time.

Dear Emma, your grandmother is going away soon and you will never see her again, she is my mother and I came out of her tummy just like you came out of my tummy and one day . . . well never mind that now . . . it is time to listen to what she has to say before she leaves. Dear Emma, these are your older brothers and they need all our help to get started in the world, and I still love you but will have to spend a lot of time with them and, look there's Daddy going to work! Dear Emma, off you go down the steps, go play with the big children on the beach before they go to school, and your cousin? Just ignore him, he's just teasing, go on, wave bye-bye to the sun, stay away from the waves, they want to take you to Neptune's Cave. Dear Emma, kiss Daddy, he is going to live with his graduate student in a snake pit and will visit you on weekends. Dear Emma, I won't tell you again, this is the last time, I've had it up to here, don't cling! you are always underfoot!

Flap flap flap. Honk honk honk.

The girl who listened to everything felt safe in vehicles, and travelled the world in perambulator and wagon and wheelbarrow and tricycle and school desk and library carrel, with and to and from her mom, smiling at everyone and then laughing, and a smile would hook a smile, a laugh would wake a laugh as pleasing as a pigeon coo. Listen. Those are mice feet; that's a crow; that's footsteps. That's a disposal unit; that's a sucker truck; that's a jet. Each crackle and scuff told her she had all the time in the world to practise words, round and fluid conversations in her head.

Because one day a boy would come, a poet explorer done with his travels, a boy with a mysterious illness, and he would be so familiar and he would give her long unhurried sentences as they crossed the Atacama, Patagonia, the Serengeti, the Rift Valley, the Gobi, Archangel on the Dvina, Tasmania, the Ghats, Bhutan, and the Olympic Peninsula, places whose names would wrap around her, impenetrable, words to hold her and catch the attention of passing hunters and gatherers pausing to tie their horses and camels and oxen and goats to stakes in remote outposts in order to converse as they traversed the plain from cities to villages.

It would take years and all her time and energy, but she wanted more than anything to find the perfect listening stance to hear such words and names, and although she did not at first recognise her long-lost cousin when he stood before her and spoke, she closed her eyes and listened, and found him, and finding him, she found it, the way to be in the speaking universe. Breath, breath, breath. Basket of ducks, basket of geese, destined for market. A herd of wild ponies. A dog backed into an alley. Her foremost self leapt. It was him!

She was his! This was possible! And then she was running, running, never stopping for more than a heart-thundering breath. *The Tao of Running, Zen of Track and Field*, her feet slap-slapping winter sidewalks and red-gravel circuits. It was him and she was skinny, hard, muscled and through the applause she would only smile and bow, smile and bow. Her background chorus of tragedy, last days, cellular exile, still sang in her blood, but now Greek was Latin, Latin was French, French was English.

Dear Emma, the desert is not empty, but he has come a long way and you only get to say the briefest hello. And these quickly erected buildings? These scaffolds, libraries, universities, museums and galleries, factories and collieries? Don't trust them, don't believe in them. They will crumble, and you will be under the sun again. Dear Emma, this is Charles. He is possible. Speak a perfect greeting. Do not stop listening and do not get fat.

Slap slap slap. Honk honk honk.

All sounds as last words. All thoughts as warnings and instructions. Charles!

3.

"Hello," he said, blocking all the light in the university cafeteria.

"Hello," she said.

"I have an olive for you," he said, and offered a plastic tub of black glistening ovals.

He was strange. He was big, tall, blue, and loud. Already he shimmered. He carried olives and a bundle of books. One book was in Latin, another in Sanskrit.

"I feel I can't say anything to you I've said before," he said, sitting down.

She was frozen. His dust in her eyes, his smell in her nose. She heard something in the soft edges of his voice that she reached for and it powdered like rust from iron, red and dry and crystalline.

"Do you want to dance?" he said.

"Here?" She felt her word waver in his direction, a wagon train, a hunting party.

"Everything seems smaller now I'm home," he said. "I've wanted to talk to you for such a long time, ever since we were children. Have another olive. What's wrong?"

She shrugged. His purple shirt was unbuttoned to show a white chest with dark springy fur, and his eyes, light blue, already danced as he leaned forward across the table. She watched him deftly shape each dangerous word, "Biology, ornithology, geology," as he stared at her. "Galapagos? No, no." He laughed and waved out of the cafeteria windows toward students on the concourse. "Or maybe I should tell you in order what has happened to me?"

She leaned away. "Sure. Everything."

"No. Not yet." He stirred a finger in the air, his eyes closed. "Let me think."

Everything because everything was swimming in silver. She wiggled her toes in the green rainy light coming through the window. She felt like dancing. She was dancing. Wiggling her toes in hard sand, the sky full of butterflies, and Charles, across from her, was explaining the dangers of mercury, the overpopulation of the world, climate change, refugia, and the near extinction of mountain gorillas and the big cats.

4.

They fixed up his house above the river where Charles watched Emma give birth to a girl, Anne, and two years later to a son, George. On the train home from the city after George, he had a dream. He and Emma were walking outside in springtime. The familiar road was wet, empty except for a gull striding along the yellow line, screaming. When he woke to the porter asking for his ticket it had rained and the sky was overcast and the woodland running the length of the tracks contained many ragged trees. He tried to make a calculation on live versus dead branches. He got stuck between separate branches and possible lives.

5.

There was a new bay window. They liked to stand together in its compass and watch the sky and the fields. Today the fields lay below a steel-grey sky. Two crows were strutting along the path. Wind scuttled rain against the window while a line of cloud brightened to the south. Emma observed and behind her Charles strode the room.

This grasp at a moment wants to make visible the transition between niche and cloister. They (we) call it a crossroad. Remission or decline, extinction or rebound? How can all that has been not be? How can faith be beside the point? What is about to happen? Repetition, like the scattered rain hitting the window, will carry them forward. Once the next scene is upon them there will be no window or rain or crows strutting or clouds brightening. The horizon may be blue to the south, but Emma will be watching her son and Charles will be climbing the stairs to the attic, where Anne, wide-mouthed and feverish, will become Annie, treacherously asleep on a galleon, free of her parents' out-loud promises, and indentured to something invisible.

6.

On Anne's first morning at school Charles got up before dawn and sat with a candle at his father's desk in the garden study and made a fist and looked at it. *And God remembered Noah.* Had God forgotten the man with all the animals? Charles looked up at his face in the window-glass. His head was never straight, it was always cocked to one side; now it was smiling. He looked like his dad. He took paper and pen out of the drawer and made a list of four things he wanted to know about himself. When he studied the list, he saw that these were not questions his wife should see even if she could answer them. He felt older than thirty-six. His face looked raw. "Why am I anxious?" was the first question. "Why do I talk like a river?" "Why do I love my daughter more than my son?" "When will I tell the thing I can't tell?"

Light showed in the east. The questions were of no use. They were unscientific. Also, the answers would stand for nothing if he answered them with no one listening. The golden September light came on snail's pace and made him feel melancholy. Human events happened too suddenly. He wanted to slow things down, live in motion slow as this light. He listened to the house. He was on a promontory, his children sleeping behind him, above him, while the travelling sun bent its patient light through the atmosphere. Over the fields, in the city, were his busy readers. He was exhausted. A moth lay dead on the floor in the dust under the desk. Of his grandparents, their parents, theirs and theirs, he knew almost nothing — only what he knew of their presence in him. The things in the room were gaining colour and edges and ordinariness. He was aware of his place among them. These things had been collected and moved from place to place through some inconceivable effort. They were his things, his and Emma's, and they would pass on to Anne and George. The light was amazing. He had built a fluid exchange between inside and outside. He could imagine his kids walking separately away into this hot darkness, through the willows into careers and mates and their own children.

After breakfast Emma and Charles walked Anne along the highway to the bus stop. The girl sat down in the shelter and would not speak and refused to stand up. Emma began to cry. Charles said he would carry the girl back to the house and drive her to school, there was time, or they could say goodbye there, or Emma could ride the bus with Anne, or — "

"It doesn't matter," Anne said. She sat straight.

Emma looked at him as if she was waiting for him to say or do something.

"One of us should go back to George," he said.

When the bus rumbled into sight Anne stood up and waved, waved the bus on, but it stopped anyway.

Emma scooped the thin girl into her arms and Charles felt stiff and upright as he watched them struggle. Eventually Emma set Anne on her feet by the rattling bus. They stood there, the three of them, in the long shadows. That's what we do, thought Charles, we turn that struggle with those we love inwards.

"I'm going to school by myself," said Anne.

She boarded the bus and Emma and Charles watched through the dirty rear window as she made her way down the aisle clutching seats to either side for balance.

7.

Emma yawned and wondered why Charles insisted on order in everything. January was the "month of our wedding," "our anniversary month," February was his birth month, and so on; and every new year she posed the question that their lives perhaps no longer fit them, expecting a discussion to follow, and perhaps a decision to pack up and move or at least a plan to travel, and all Charles did was build onto the house — his study jutting into the garden when his first book took off, last year the bay window, and what would it be this year? They were comfortable, but she was restless.

She looked at him writing notes in the margin of a typed page. His mouth was open. She was fascinated by his mouth. She seldom noticed his eyes. Perhaps that would be it, a few more stories, a little renovation every year. They always argued about it. What he wanted, what she wanted. He spoke, she contradicted. Sometimes she spoke, but he never listened. She couldn't keep her thoughts on track. This house was almost aquatic in the spring, the birdsong fishsong. And the sound of rain was like Noah's final lecture.

The wind was freshening. And here they were analysing their relationship in terms of what could happen next. Or she was analysing; he was pretending to think, his pen poised. The windows contained green hills, rippled and distorted. George, dressed in his rain cape had just come in and was squeaking along the blue tiles. He was struggling with the heavily sprung bathroom door. Soon would be lunchtime.

She'd tell the children the story of Noah this afternoon. She'd told it all before, variations on why, what and how. Why did the Lord flood the world? What had we done that was so wicked? How could it rain so much? According to Charles, there had been a single cataclysmic event. Nature throwing in a wrench, dipping an oar, tightening a screw. With Charles, her silence on God was unsilent. Couldn't he just float out his theories and allow her her belief every now and then? While he read and scrawled and chewed his pen, the clouds rolled away. Everything in their vicinity was dripping; the sun came out; George came out of the washroom across the hall. He looked shocked, worried, pleased, puzzled, interested, and dazed, in that order. And Emma burrowed deeper into her thoughts and tried not to disturb Charles.

The sun illuminated his face and his open mouth. What was he thinking? She reached and hit him on the shoulder. "It's lunchtime. If you want a sandwich, go and get one."

And obediently he wandered off. He disappeared for an hour.

She bent her head and drank in the gorgeous plumage of the carpet. Charles was still good-looking, youthful. Just last week she had admired his back as she watched him set the first stone of his wall, after years of gathering and crouching and pondering, his fool-work, and now he was like a runaway, outside scouting direction at every opportunity, a master of escaping her questions.

She felt his attention on her and looked up. "What's wrong?"

"Annie has had a hard fall. She's soaked. She was at the farm getting patched up."

"Is she all right?"

"I think so. She's getting changed."

8.

"How are you today?" he asked.

The girl lay pale under the skylight, just awake. Last night had been worse than the night before. She had had her second fever. No medicine would help. He had drunk too much wine. They had sent George to his grandparents. He had had with Emma incomplete sex and now he was upstairs in Annie's bedroom feeling guilty.

"I'm okay, Papa."

"Will I tell you a story?"

"Yes, please."

Afterward he went downstairs to the front room where Emma stood looking out of the bay window. She turned as soon as she heard him. "How is she?"

He shook his head. "When she's sick I can't think."

Emma sank into her chair. She played with the worn threads of the armrest. "Are you afraid, Charles? Are you afraid?"

"They bury themselves in the sand."

"Who do?"

"The San. The original humans, according to genetic research. The folk who stayed in Africa when the rest of us left. To escape the heat. What d'you think are our chances of understanding life before our grandchildren come along?"

She looked away from him. "Please don't start."

"All creatures seek water, but only at certain times of the day. When it is safe. What if knowledge is water? We don't really know who we are or why we're here, do we?"

She flinched. She wrinkled her nose. She craned her neck, gazing through the bay window, fingers busy with the worn armrest. "Our kids are good, aren't they?"

He went to the window to see what she was looking at. The road outside was wet, empty except for a gull striding along, big red screams leaving its beak. "She will be okay."

"I'm afraid now, Charles."

"She will be fine, sweetheart."

"But she's worse, isn't she, Charles?"

"Yes."

"She woke me up in the night. When I went into her room, she was soaking wet."

"She's sleeping now."

9.

The April walk through the field path was a last goodbye. Their sweet child was gone, and they were daily overflown by Canada geese. He dared not touch his wife.

"When did the light begin to fade?" he said. "Was it that first year in the city, when we began misunderstanding each other? Is it our fault? Do you know?"

"I don't want you to do this now. You want to offend God and I want to praise Him."

"I mean no offence. I can only blame nature and myself. I only have questions."

"You ask stupid questions. I think you've never considered me. Most of the time you are in your own world. You don't care about me."

"I don't ask stupid questions."

"All right."

"Are you actually interested in hearing what I think?"

"Not much any more. Most of it has nothing to do with anyone. Listening to you is exhausting. It's a sort of constant useless exercise."

"Do you want me to stop talking to you?"

"It was Annie's time. She loved Jesus."

"That doesn't help me."

"We are breaking down, Charles. We need to be with others. I feel so heavy today," she said. "And yet life's going on. We're not getting anywhere, are we? Let's go back."

They had ceased. They had stopped halfway. Where was the path? Emma was panting, her mouth open. There would be no greater challenge. Probably for both of them. The geese were so loud. Probably it was her fault. Perhaps his heart was failing. He felt her weight leaving his side, her body crossing the field, going away. He watched her draw the shawl over her hair. Her shoulders were wet.

"Wait."

Through the trees the windows of the house reflected green and sky. He felt they were the only passengers. And she was leaving him. Clouds were massed to the west. Women struggled with God, that heavily sprung idea. *Déjà vu?*

"Wait! I have something to say."

10.

They were returning to the house. She was trying to breathe. She'd listen to him now, even though she'd heard it all before, or variations, because she had to hang onto something and his voice was a life-line. He spoke, she listened. And if she had never really listened before, never really heard, did it matter? She was listening now. She wouldn't contradict him. God had thrown in His wrench, dipped His oar, tightened His screw. Her silence was silent. He was eloquent. Incredible. Like birds calling. Like ravens calling. Incredible. Let him converse with the hedge-dwellers, the shaw-birds, in their vicinity. Let him charm wrens from their thicket. Each quick, suspicious, pleased, puzzled wren. She was inside and outside at once. She was between rooms. She burrowed deeper into herself as the sun illuminated his face, his talking mouth. She could see all his years of hovering and crouching over rocks and fossils, all the seas he'd crossed. He had built his stories and now he was breaking them down for her. He was like a derailed train. She was fascinated. The split world was full and mobile, even though it was poisoned. They shouldn't have sent George away. That haze was from the fire in the death room. What a beautiful pearly light in the smoke. Opalescent.

"Of course we keep going because we are following our desire. I am following my desire to speak and you are following the desire to listen. The geese follow the seasons and the seasons . . . "

What was he? She turned and struck his chest with her fist.

11.

He shrank back, told her she looked like the graceful statue of Mary she kept on her dresser. He knew the longer he talked and the longer she listened the quicker time would fly. And he could always find, after all, something to say, especially now she had given up trying not to listen.

"We are confused," he said, "by the uncertainty that ensues when long-held patterns of behaviour are interrupted. It's not just us. So many of these birds — thrushes, robins, wrens, tits, finches — are in trouble. The latest mist-netting fieldwork and point-counts tell of coming extinctions. Listen to those crows. The Bushmen's language follows the calls of birds . . . "

She bent her head. "Annie's hair was so soft and fine."

He drank her in. She was still good-looking, though no longer youthful. "There is a filled niche — no room for listening or talking — when Eros is in the room. No one truly dies."

"Charles? What's happening?"

He felt her attention on him. He studied her. She tilted away toward the house.

This was frightening. He was frightened. He leaned forward and kissed her ear.

12.

"Was I asleep?"

"Oh, just for an hour."

They were upstairs in Annie's room. Emma lay on the bed under the skylight. Last night the house had been empty all over again.

"How do you feel today?"

"I am trying, Charles, but it makes no sense. How are you?"

"Not good. Not so good."

"I depend on you, you know."

"You want me to worship."

"I don't."

"I can't do it, Emma."

Again he saw her weight shift before she turned over and slid out of Annie's bed. She crossed the room. He watched her draw the curtains back.

"The sun is so red," she said. "What time is it?"

"Nearly seven."

"That's haze from the city, I suppose. What a light in the sky. Pearly pink . . . ."

She stayed a long time at the window. He stood guard.

"What was it you said? *Once a niche is filled, then Eros looks for a change?*"

"That's just the way it is."

13.

But now she'd stopped listening. She was the mother who had given birth to the children of this man and she couldn't remember how she had got to where she was, where she was, who was around her, or what he was. Let him talk to others, she didn't want to witness it.

"I have been pregnant and in labour and now I have lost a child." She took his hand and set it on her belly. "What happens if I deny God? I will never repair this."

"We must bring George home," he said.

"Yes, we must get George home."

14.

That summer, Emma's hopelessness was complete and overarching. That summer Charles built the glass schoolroom and in the fall their first students enrolled.

"You wanted the school," Charles said, "and I wanted to make you forget."

"The children are still not settled. They are wary of us."

"Oh, come on. Of me, you mean."

"Charles, you're only interested in sitting at your desk. We need to be useful to others."

"It's not fair on George."

George, unless he was asleep, would not stay still. He never stopped running, inside and outside the house. His constant running was from Charles to Emma, from Emma to Charles. And then he began running away from home. The day he turned eighteen he sat his mother down in the glass room to say he was going away, like Uncle Danny, and they had small conversations all through the day about his prospective travels. She found that her son had always thought he was a little safe boat in the midst of chaos. Everything since Annie had been out of hand, almost too much. Now it was almost in hand he was going away. Charles, who was busy most days at his wall, joined them in the late afternoon.

The three of them sat together in the garden.

Charles told them a story of three kings and two crowns and a magic wagon full of words that fell off a bridge into a chasm.

Emma said nothing.

George asked why didn't the kings invent a system to share the crowns?

They were busy men with kingdoms to run. Or it didn't occur to them.

"What good is a kingdom?" Emma said.

"What good are words?" her son asked.

"Ask your father."

15.

Charles brought Emma a gin and tonic.

"Our son will come down that road, along that path, one day very soon."

"What if he doesn't come?"

"We can't imagine otherwise."

"Why not?"

"Ah." He turned his back on the wind, sat in the tall grass, lay down.

"No, Charles, please don't. I can't see you."

"Can you see me now?" He raised a hand and knew his five fingers were visible at the same level as the hissing seed heads. The sky so big and blue up there.

"Yes."

"Is he in sight yet?"

"Not yet."

"Tell me when you see the dust." He was down there because of tears and not wanting to be seen crying. Her dress was so old and thin a teardrop would dissolve the cotton. The stems stood as straight as thin pale legs.

"It's all right, Charles. I'm okay."

Of course she was okay. He'd made the renovations, built the glass school; the wall was a few feet long. What next? He would rise in a moment and walk up to the house. He would go back to the house and leave Emma.

16.

He was alone in the garden as usual at the end of the day. Afraid. For a moment Emma was a cloud covering the sun. *This was where we sat with George when he told us. No, no. That was another hillside. This one faces south. Been here before, though. No. No.* Annie was dead and he didn't know whether his son was alive or dead.

Charles.

What.

Charles?

Yes?

He was writing a tale about a house by the sea where an old man watched birds fly from their cliff nests into the air. The old man would pop out his hearing aids and enter silence, the mass of undigested memories low in his gut, and watch the eerie birds swaying out over the mute surf and back. *What are words? Where do they come from? What are they?*

Words are what we use to talk of where we have been and who we are.

I can see you!

Is he coming yet?

Not yet.

He felt the planet tilt, the raw words rising through his chest: Sanskrit, Persian, Latin, English. In the end Emma understood nothing except what he told her. Annie thanked him for the water. It didn't matter that she was his daughter. When she died, Emma was holding her hand and Emma's old friends were calling.

Gulls were crying above the nuisance grounds. *His* old friends calling. Okay. He would rise in a moment and leave the wall and go back to the house. No, no running away. There was a light in the clouds, through the clouds, yes, and down below — this was memory, surely, all memory — down under the ground he'd discovered an old wooden wheel. Uncover the grass, lift the brown thatch and there would be the rim, chipped blue paint, and the spokes. A girl's voice was calling, listen, over there, far away, calling to a dog or horse or brother. The wheel if unearthed would be missing spokes. The wheel of an old wagon or carriage. It was not so important to hear what the girl was calling. The hillside was a swaying green down to the road, but he didn't want to return all the way home until the light in the sky changed and the wheel was pushed down a bit farther. Because this wheel was what mattered, not the top, which had been in the wind, not the hidden part, but the whole wheel: this half-buried wheel with only the girl's voice, not insistent yet, disturbing the stillness.

Who can I talk to now? Blue flakes on the rim, the hub in darkness, Annie's scraped knees, curling hair, without meaning, this spring without meaning, wet spring, and yet her spirit will flavour next year, along with a few ideas — how to count the earthworms pushing into starlight; that's something Emma and I can talk about, knowing we are ordinary, knowing nothing but our children, remembered bits of childhood, that nun, that shopping list that went treasure, treasure, treasure, treasure, don't forget the milk, there are children in the house. *But not for long. The hub divided into centuries when we could say centuries before we knew things took millennia to change. Olives in brine. Now there's no one to take one and none to offer and no one to listen and the wheel was a story once, the rust quick on the tongue. Be still. There's no one to listen. What might I say? Summer, yes, fall, yes. One by one the spokes forget who they are next to.*

MISTRESS OF HORSES, MISTRESS OF THE SEA

Oft denk' ich, sie sind nur ausgegangen,
bald werden sie wieder nach Hause gelangen.

Friedrich Rückert
(from *Kindertotenliede*)

I

1.

I wish I had a simpler voice. I had one once, when I was young. My thoughts have too many angles now. This river valley is rich. I can appreciate its opulence from the shelter of my wall this late afternoon, raindrops falling from a low cloud, its smell and colours and little winds. But our village is slipping. We are waning in population, our discards outweigh our possessions. True. What else? A smoke would keep me from falling asleep. I pat my pockets and look out for my wife returning from Dmitri's Market. She trades as best she can with her arm in a sling. Such a fine wholesome gentle woman to anchor me to the earth's molten core despite Danny's horses, specks in the distance, cropping the curly grass below the vine hills, between the field of stooks and the orange river. Apocat and Kata sit near the river in a haze of dust kicked up by the rain, dry under the big tree where they weave their lazy baskets. This is their job: to weave at the edge of things as the world convulses and the village slips beneath the waves, just as Emma's job is to give me ballast and my job is to report the faults in the facts that let in the dreams. I am still recording, though not broadcasting, as if redundant, as if silent and have nothing more to say to the outer world, even though these horses go on cropping, a wife shops at market, wise women weave, even though summer rain fattens the grapes. Ah, but is there a new element? Something between horse and sea, axe and tree? What exactly is it?

The people still gather at the edges of their yards and chatter before the sun goes down. The village has thrived another day. We've kept our noses to the ground. And today I feel excited and guilty. What is it? I felt such apprehension as I watched Abi, Tom's teen daughter, and Danny riding off together between the rows of vines and disappearing north.

Response to my first novel of some thirty years ago encouraged me to continue to record details of village life and to send these away, and in fact I have in my possession the letter I received from a professor who recognized the value of my writing, stating that in order to maintain a purity of narrative — a clean line, he called it — the river should flow only one way, and signing his name, "with respect from future generations." Well, I sent out stories for years. All were published. I wrote and floated them down the river until Annie died, when suddenly I felt I was engaging in a species of betrayal and stopped transmitting. It's important to say that I did not stop writing in my notebooks.

I have had a life of local exploration and storytelling and have anchored that life in the relationships with my wife and children. These relationships too became subject to exploration and story. But now I find myself looking over the village, full of my customary curiosity, still witnessing stunningly vivid people engaged in beautiful affairs (this includes my wife; night-dreams of my children are a separate reality), and yet my longhand copy of these people and their affairs seems a dead thing. So what has happened? Have my tools become blunt or is my approach obsolete? Would another looking at my notebooks find all well and interesting and simply *finished, complete, perfect*? Am I finished? Or is the problem in the village — am I the witness to a *discontinuity* that is not translatable by means I've used before? Am I aware of continuity behind the discontinuity for the first time? I have set my stock in evolution and seen it everywhere around me, and the world and my village have supported my certainty, which is not a belief, surely, because it is provable. It is provable. A long time ago I discovered two options of pursuing a graceful perceptive narrative, either by being faithful to the characters, or to wring a poem from the moment. Or let a poem wring from me a transcendent copy of the moment. The options blur, of course. It has often been a combination of these approaches, but now I have a nagging suspicion the options are front and back, top and bottom of an uncrackable nut.

Two months ago, I came upon a doe by the side of the road, killed by some impact, and she was large, with young within her slowly dying. I stopped and looked at her and spoke to her, but I did not touch her, and I feel badly that I did not. Annie died, our daughter, and she is still slowly dying, inside Emma, inside me. Some impact. Some agency. A vector that we overlooked, that has been filled with guilt, that that that . . . So what happened? If evolution is just one story, if time and space don't hold, what then? And here is where dreams enter in, when our son George says I might be wrong about everything, and young Annie, bright as ever, arrives to say none of it really matters anyway.

"One cannot live in a constant state of fear," says Kata.

"Who is not afraid?" says Apocat. She settles her bulk tenderly, everything slow with her these days, beneath the big tree, and the whole settlement shifts a degree north and sun breaks out of a black cloud.

"I will tell you who is full of fear and who is full of rage," says Kata.

"Who?"

"Abi and Danny."

"Ah."

"That girl has lives to live before her baby can be born. And his illness will lead him into terrible places."

Apocat sighs. "Will you fetch me a drink of water, Kata."

Kata scurries to the bucket and dips the scoop and fills a tin cup. Down on her haunches, she turns and raindrops spit around her. "Who is to blame, the girl or the man?"

Apocat shakes her shaggy grey head. "Why do we have to blame?"

"Well, it's not our fault, is it?" says Kata.

"We can't blame the village, can we?" says Apocat. "Like the old days?"

"No, no." Kata brings the tin cup. "I think Danny's anger is a roof and Abi's fear needs a home."

"Good, Kata. That's a good start."

∽

I used to enjoy watching the comings and goings of babies with their mothers, kids on skateboards in the alleys, toddlers with balloons, on tricycles, but now it's mostly teens swaggering along the summer lanes to the vineyards, Gee and James for instance, the latest young lovers roaming up the vine hills for a private spot and down when they're done. I imagine them the way I enjoy brandy, a little too much.

Emma does not know. We have kept secret from each other all these years who we truly are. We avoid talking about Annie. When I die, all my notes and observations may well be added up, though I'm afraid it won't amount to much. When I think of all the long-empty houses with their off-kilter Sold signs, I feel dizzy and go out to set a rock in my wall.

When one does something over and over it becomes a path to one's own soul, complete with smells and visions and associated thoughts. Our village is diminished and under threat. How does a diminished village affect its inhabitants? I might as well ask the stone how it is affected by the wall.

Backache.

Fused discs.

Calm, calm.

Papagana.   Pabbivinnar.   Ayabmenang.   Apanyer. Vatergewinnt. Babamafanikio. The play names I once gave my children to give me wobble in my lips only now, when I'm lost, when I'm sad, their big shouty laughter a beat away.

It's already dusk, and the villagers are out in their yards, chatting back and forth. I cannot see them because our house stands apart from the village and faces the vine hills. But it is a still evening and the voices are distinct. Stars grow visible one by one, cluster by cluster; laughter winds round and round the bulky darkness until, one after another, the voices go silent and the night breeze comes up. Out there on the outskirts is the young and beautiful couple in the tent pitched outside the community hall. They are not what they seem. I have asked James and Gee and Abi and Harry, who have made it a habit since summer began to pass the tent every day, afraid of missing something, what they are like. "Cool." "Smart."

"Boring." "Interesting." These kids are finished Grade 9 and have first jobs, Abi looking after Danny's horses, Harry washing dishes at the diner, Gee clerking at the dress shop, and James on Abi's dad's farm.

☙

"What's it all about?" says James.

"We want to be close to the ground," the woman says.

"We want to feel the weather," the man says.

"What do you do?" says Gee.

"Sleep and work," he says.

"What kind of work?"

"We're ethnologists."

"Students," his partner corrects.

"Can you cook in there?"

"We'll put in a stove and chimney for the winter."

"It looks small," says Abi.

"Yeah," says James.

"Inside it's huge," says the man.

"It doesn't seem big," says Harry.

"It has rooms," says the woman.

"No way," says Gee.

"Check it out." He unzips the front and the kids lean in.

"Wow. It does have rooms."

"Sure."

"Cool," says Harry.

"What's the point?" says James.

☙

This young man and woman sit outside their tent drinking coffee early in the morning, then wander around the village

~ 106 ~

most of the day. They shop at Dmitri's store, interview select villagers at the hall in the evening. They have been given keys to the meeting room and bathrooms and showers. They aren't kids; they aren't adults. They call themselves researchers, ethnographers. Abi and Gee and James and Harry say they wouldn't mind living in a tent, but would never choose their own village to do it in.

∾

"Is something happening?" Harry asks.

"What d'you mean?" says Gee.

"I mean to the village. Why are they really here?"

"Let's go ask 'em," says James.

"Let's not," says Abi.

She feels a wave of heat when James takes Gee's hand. Harry follows. Then they all wade through the high grass, snapping seed heads.

The woman sits crosslegged on a cushion and the guy sprawls with his legs stretched out on a red carpet on the ground.

"Is something going on here we don't know about?" says Gee.

"For sure," says the guy.

"What?"

"You've heard of the quarry they want to build?"

"Yeah," says James. "It'll never happen."

"That's what we want to find out," says the woman. "What you all think."

"If you know something," Harry says, "you must tell us."

"No, no. We make a hypothesis," says the woman, "then we ask questions."

"We'll answer questions," says James.

"Or are we the wrong people to ask?" says Harry.

"Are you all bored?" the guy asks. He is staring at Abi.

"Yeah!" they all say.

"We know a lot about village life," says Gee. "It is no big deal. This place is really dead."

It's quiet then, just crows calling, Abi scanning the faces.

Gee says: "But you don't know what goes on in people's lives really. Only what they tell you."

"I'm not really bored," says Abi.

"No," says Harry. "I think everything is . . . important."

"What about you?" the woman asks James.

"Yeah, bored," says James. "Bored means bored."

I take our little dog, Polly, along the river so I can think and we meet the black dog with three legs and Polly growls. There are dogs and dogs. There are young and old. There is birth after birth. What is evolution but reincarnation plus space/time? Infer, remember. What do tent-dwellers portend? Do these tent-dwellers herald a new nomadism? The three-legged dog runs up to Apocat and Kata who are weaving baskets on the reedy bank; the green stream purls and winks; the old women wave; all my thoughts scatter. I wave back, a storyteller with no plot, short-distance traveller, and call Polly. Polly looks up and wags her tail and we go home.

My wife's arm is broken. Emma can't sleep the night through and her pain wakes us both. She was drunk. She got drunk with Danny. Not yet, not yet. To tell a story before its time is like hooking a fish before the river has found its bed. It is possible, but no meanders live here yet.

Peaceful breakfast and a cup of tea by the wall amid summer's alarming gold; Polly losing herself in the river grass, chasing small animals. But even that quick story has its twists and turns I'm too old or drowsy to pursue and investigate. I've had no human dialogue except with Emma for weeks of sleepless nights, during which I whisper to the dark, more prayer than story. I will pause here and consider the shale at the river's edge where I stood this morning watching Polly forage. *Children are scarce.* Only Tom's family seems to be having them. What else? *Tolerate repetition; welcome interruption; build the wall.* Nomads no less, nomads in a tent. What have I done with my life? I'm husband to a broken arm and friend of subtle differences, jealous of Shakespeare, envious of Chuang Tzu, perplexed by Sankara, and I want the finished shirt before the cotton has been picked and expect slavery before my dad's father beat his dog.

2.

"You should see the coast of British Columbia," Danny says. He is an old man telling a story in a barn, all shadows and surging light. He is not really her uncle even though she's known him forever; he is her employer. He has been showing her what she has to do and soon they'll take a couple of horses out. "The sea began a discontent in me. I wasn't much older than you. On leave I met a married woman a lot older than me and we fell in love." He leans against a stall, eyes far away. "I need a coffee. You want a coffee?"

"Okay."

On their way up to the house, he gets out of breath. "I can ride, but walking's a bitch."

"Are you okay?" she asks.

"Yeah. Just a little pain. I don't like the heat. I'm fine."

After coffee they ride. Out into the vines. Starlings loud and fluid in the sky.

Abi reins in. "How old were you when you fell in love?"

"Nineteen," he says, strain in his voice. "She was thirty-three. She had kids."

"Did she?"

"Yeah. Two girls."

"What happened?"

"She left her husband."

"She left her girls?" Abi says. "That's wild. Then what?"

The sun vanishes behind a cloud and hot wind gusts against them and the land beyond the vines looks twitchy, then dull.

He takes a minute to blink and gaze around him. "I remember spending a whole afternoon in an apple tree, shaking the branches, and she was on the ground, catching what fell, just like a kid. She had horses. We were going to make a run for it." He raises himself in the stirrups and points. "Beyond those hills, past the reserve, is the pass. The landrace ponies still live in a high valley behind there. And we did make a short run, but she went back to him, so no, in the end she didn't leave her children."

They sit their horses a while in the warm wind then ride slowly back through the grape hills, the vines hanging limp, rain ticking among the leaves.

∾

"They're gypsies. Impermanent, untrustworthy," says Tom.

"Because they live in a tent?" says Lucy. "They're just students."

"I don't like the way they dress or the way they talk. They're phony. They're up to no good. They have no values."

"I think they do."

"Have you spoken to them?"

"I've said hello. They seem fine young people. And Abi's down there all the time. Just because they're educated—"

"Abi's supposed to be working."

"She is working. You've talked to them, Tom?"

"No. But I've studied them some. I've heard stories.

"From who?"

"From Charles."

"Give me a break."

"They're up to no good. They're gypsies."

Perhaps they have come looking for me. Hubris. I didn't send for them. I'd have ordered people less sure of themselves. Their knowledge of our geography and plants and animals is impressive and they have the Latin names for everything. They sleep in their tent on the hall land at the edge of the village — on what used to be called common land — and are proud, self-important, beautiful. They point recorders and cameras at everything. They hound Apocat and Kata, making notes, taking photographs. The first time they came to the house Emma was out so I made them tea, though I'd rather have spent time with a pair of layabouts who liked to drink and sing songs and had no equipment. Breathless young gods, they made me breathless, and it was intoxicating to look at them, for they didn't acknowledge anything outside themselves, not really. The glances they shared with each other, let me say, contained crates of condescension. What hunger! What clothes! What bodies!

"Mr Darwin, your stories will form a cornerstone of our research paper," said the young woman.

"Call me Charles."

"She's trying to flatter you," said the young man.

She said, "I mean it's all good, Charles. We'd like to do interviews, then use the old stories as a sort of map."

"What do you mean?"

She laughed. "Atavism, as irruptive balance to the modern world."

"Decline of the economic world," he said.

"Post post post," she said.

"That's our bag, our lens," he said.

"Our lens," she echoed.

I had no idea why they were in my back yard. The sun had shifted and the shade was vanishing. "Are you looking for evidence of general failure?"

They both laughed this time.

"We're not detectives," she said. "We are participant observers. We want to observe this village for the summer, maybe a year, if we can get funding."

The young man said: "It's a matter of sorting out. We need to sort manifest signifiers into pre-conscious and unconscious streams."

She shrugged. "You know what is on your horizon?" There she was, gazing, not soulfully but critically, at that painfully familiar horizon.

"No." How annoying all this was. I'd been happily sizing up the next rock for my wall. Soon it would be too hot to work. What did they want from me?

"You represent a route to the source," he said. "The way things used to be. Well, the stories."

"'The Grasslands Beneath the Vines,' for instance," she said.

"Yes, exactly," he said.

She said, "Do you know that neural currents and autonomic responses to immunological memory transcend in data volume all events in history and prehistory?"

"Even the most awful reversals," he said. "Neural plasticity is the tip of the iceberg, and the iceberg is part of the easy problem."

While I pretended calm, they talked about the immune system, the nervous system, the old human brain, the hard problem of consciousness.

"A hundred generations before *The Origin of the Species*," she said, "Maori facial tattoos were mapping battle paths through English landscapes." She screwed up her face and giggled. "We're talking to Charles Darwin."

"So, we will live with you," he said. "Hopefully, we will stay a year and get involved in all you do."

They seemed immune to the hot sun. They seemed on the edge of laughter. Were they serious? Who on earth had their teachers been? They didn't even know their way into each other, though they were randy. That showed in the shirts and shorts, in the way they did everything backwards, their fingers and lips trembling. Her glassy-eyed spouting, his lanky acerbity. They were know-it-all dragons from some ecstatic future hunting a big bang they'd misplaced in the clutter of procedural notes. That's not me, by the way, that's them. It must be contagious. At last they left and I went inside and lay on the cool tiles in the glass room to calm the shooting pains in my back.

All August I have watched them bounce through our village, ranting about *naturalistic explanations, redundant vernacular,* chasing their *manifest signifiers.*

∾

"Abi's terrified," says Kata.

"What have young girls to do with fear?" Apocat rustles her heels in the scattered reeds. She leans against the tree, shuts her eyes.

Kata snaps her fingers. "She is a seedpod! A seedpod! Are you listening?"

Apocat groans. "Let's not get ahead of ourselves."

"And nothing will touch Daniel's rage."

Apocat rubs her spine into rough bark. When she cracks her eyelids to the low red sun, she spies the slinking three-legged dog. "All men dream of such girls. What do you make of that dog, Kata?"

Kata stretches her neck and squawks. "That dog's sending more signals than a bucketful of snakes."

"Yes. It's hungry . . . "

"For goodness' sake." Kata leans forward and shouts: "The days are getting shorter. The ditch must be crossed."

"I don't know . . . " Apocat sighs. "I don't know."

"By the dead and the living."

"Oh, my feet hurt." Apocat pulls off and flexes each of her worn-out sandals. "These must be fixed."

3.

The four kids wander the edge of town along the river path until it dips below the bank. They emerge, climb up to the hall, and join the ethnographers on the red carpet outside their tent. The young woman brews tea and they all sit together.

"You figuring us out yet?" says James.

"Yes."

"What do you do in your tent?"

"The usual things," the man says.

"Cook, clean and collate," says the woman, smiling brightly.

"We think it's crazy," says Gee, "what you're doing."

They sip their tea in silence. The carpet fits into the centre of a rectangle of dead grass. Vultures wheel high above.

"We don't really understand," says Harry.

Abi says, "I looked it up. You compare people."

"Peoples," the guy corrects. "We are socio-cultural anthropologists. Aren't we?"

"Not really," his partner says. "We're students."

"What will you be when you grow up?" says James.

They all laugh.

∽

Our village is young but there was an earlier village. And one before that. People have lived here by the river for a long time. They say the plain to the north is sacred. When Danny and I turned eighteen we were supposed to go travelling together, to see the world. We'd been friends through school, since we were small. We had compared the arrowheads and small flint tools we'd found. We'd saved for years for our travels. But after graduation he had a girlfriend and I didn't and that divided us, and when Danny bought a motorcycle, expecting me to do the same, I was already buying land — a tumbledown house on a piece of bench above the river where I planned to catalogue all the flora and fauna within sight of the windows — and I used my savings as a down payment and with my parents' help began to fix the crumbling shell into this house Emma and I live in now. Danny and his girl rode his motorcycle away and she came back alone a few months later. By the time he returned, we were in our mid twenties and I was married, with two children, and he was wild, rabid, and had rotten teeth. We met on occasion, but could barely tolerate each other.

~

Abi answers the door and leads Gee up to her room.

"Your house smells so weird," Gee says. "It smells like something died."

"No it doesn't."

"So what's the deal with Harry? Are you guys dating or what?"

"He's just a friend. Nothing's going on. What about you and James?"

"He's so depressed. No way. No thanks."

They sit in Abi's room, crosslegged on the floor, trading song lyrics. Abi's mother appears with a plate of cookies and two glasses of milk.

"Thanks, Lucy," Gee says. "How's the baby?"

Lucy folds her hands over her belly. "About ready," she says. "You enjoying the dress shop?"

"Oh yes, very much," says Gee.

"You'll be back at school in a couple of weeks. Grade 10! Looking forward to it?"

"Oh yes, I can't wait to see all my friends."

When the door closes, Gee turns to Abi. "I'd kill my mother if she walked into my room with cookies and milk. What are we, six?" She bites into her cookie, then waves her hand in the air. "So, what about those guys?"

"In the tent?"

"Yeah. Are they, like, together?"

"He's smart isn't he?"

"Who cares?"

"I suppose I do," says Abi. "I don't think he's as smart as she is."

"I mean they are together, obviously, but . . . " Gee rolls onto her back. "You see him checking us out?"

"His girlfriend, or whatever she is, is really pretty."

"She's one of those smart bitches — you can tell. He's not really into her, you can tell. What are they really doing here?"

"Like they said, research. She said it's a PhD thesis."

"About this shit place? I don't buy it. Hey, wanna go hang out down there?" She holds her fingers laced above her face and squints. "I got some weed."

Abi leans against the bed and stares out the window. "In a little while, maybe."

"I like your room," says Gee. "But what's that colour?" she points at the wall.

"Eggshell."

"Eggshell?"

"We're more interesting than our parents," says Abi.

"No doubt."

"I really want to live someplace else. I don't think I can wait."

"Yeah. I hate this place. Me and James both."

∽

Danny wasn't the first to try the world. Once upon a time, villagers travelled to France and China and India and America and Brazil and Africa and Australia and Japan and many came back, though not all. Villagers journeyed with Bodhidharma's thoughts and returned with new bodies and souls; stopped a night on the banks of the Nile on the way home from Jerusalem and shared water with Mohammed; met Lao Tzu on the tenth week of his self-exile and brought home new ideas and precious-fangled tools. We have been monks and saints. We have been profligate and fruitful. Hearts stopped in wars, and from every death sprouted a dozen sons and daughters. Most of us stayed here, growing grapes for trade and small crops for ourselves, and there was a golden time. Now more and more go away, fewer and fewer children are born; entropy is upon us, the end of a cycle, and we are half-metal and nearly complete. Ambition and loss to the utmost.

∽

Abi and Gee run downstairs and out, down to the river and along.

"James is working," says Gee. "Where's Harry?"

"At the diner," says Abi. "He works and sleeps, never does anything else."

Gee rolls a joint and they get stoned, then paddle off a sandbar into the green water.

"Yeah, me and James think they have kinky sex, that couple."

"So what?"

"Probably have kinky sex all the time."

"Why is it green?" says Abi.

"It's poisonous," says Gee. "My dad says they're dumping waste upriver, those mines?"

"No, it's from the trees."

"From the light," says Gee. "The light is green."

"I think the water's green first," says Abi.

"Reflected from the trees," says Gee. "You think he's good looking?"

"Who?"

"Harry."

"Kinda not. He's not bad."

"He's so dumb."

"He's just shy."

"So critical and straight all the time."

"Do you believe in yourself, Gee?"

"Of course I do."

"I don't think I do."

Abi hikes up through the brush to the dead grass of the hall land. She stands in green light and looks at the blue tent, and at the tent reflected in the hall's big glass windows.

Everything green, green and quiet, except for the man, who is wearing a white shirt with the sleeves rolled up. He waves. Abi goes over and they chat. He offers her a cup of tea.

They sit on the carpet in front of the tent. They both know this is like the other time, the time not mentioned, that time.

"How d'you know what's important and what's not?" she asks.

"We don't," he says. Beautiful dark neck in the white shirt. Dark muscular arms. He is teasing her. He wants her to guess, to keep asking questions. Lean and restless. Amber eyes, almost. Hazel-brown. A bony man, big knees.

"You just record everything?"

"That's right."

"Then what?"

"Transcribe, study, think. Look for inconsistencies."

"Inconsistencies?"

"Yeah."

They sit in the hot sun, flies circling their cups. She feels him looking at her. Sweat trickles down her back. The woman is away from the tent, just like the other time. Harry and James are at work. Gee is down by the river. There's only a little shade and her legs are burning. Long and brown. Where he is looking.

∽

When Danny and I were thirty the farmers were competing to produce the perfect grape, and Apocat and Kata were noticing the absence of songbirds. That's when I started publishing.

Danny's parents are dead and my father's dead and Mother despairs of anything new, and Danny and I are approaching sixty. My father was a stone and remembered every detail of the past (my failures, et cetera), and my mother, sand, remembers nothing, but follows precisely every bird's chirp and trill, and every breeze-blown leaf and feather outside her windows.

The threadbare streets seem even more desolate now, with that couple wandering around. How is it all connected? How will it all play out? I go too fast. Before packing up my tools, I need to think back to Danny's homecoming thirty-five years ago.

He'd been living on the sea, a sailor, had alien ways of speaking and couldn't stop talking about a lover, a married woman who said she would give up everything for him, but in the end could not leave her children. It took him a long time to settle. His parents wanted him to live at home with them, but he refused. He acquired a couple of horses, slept in his father's cabin outside the village and refused to work with his father and uncles, would not discuss grape growing and wine making, spent all his waking hours on the reserve or riding with the landrace ponies that were then pushing at the walls of our vineyards. He talked about the sea and the woman and horses, though nobody but me really listened. He said that the sea respected him, but women hated him and only horses loved him, the ponies who were exiles like him, of course, inbred and selected over centuries — and he would go on for hours about a lost valley beyond the pass, cut off from the world, isolated from humans.

Apocat and Kata were young women just settled in town, with nothing to do but cut their eyes at this young pungent strange altered village man.

These days, while the sisters track Danny's advancing illness, I wonder how far village fortunes will dip before we rise from our beds into a new equilibrium. It's unthinkable, death; Danny, if I know him, will not slip so easily toward his own. Death, I suppose, is always a new darkness, always interesting. A month ago my wife Emma tried, under Danny's regime, to ride a young mustang and fell and broke her arm, almost her back. She was drunk, a painful, other story. I said that. She could have died.

∾

"Something stinks!" Kata screeches.

"What?" says Apocat.

"I said something stinks."

"The sea, is it again? I'm all stuffed up. It's all this dust."

"No, not the sea. But you had a bad dream last night. You said thick ice covered everything and it was the end of our village."

"Did I, Kata? I'm afraid I don't remember."

∾

To expect the weavers by the river to solve the village's future is futile. My wife's arm is mending but she can't sleep the night through without being woken by pain.

True of me, too, what Abi said. I don't believe in myself either. I loved hearing my name spoken by my parents, though seldom heard it. Danny was a beautiful youth and he made sense of me, but I was bullied by the kids at school, who called me stupid, moron, goofy. I looked in a mirror and wanted no part of me. Not that ugly boy, not that shame-filled boy. There were days so bleak they felt like the end of time, though buds were on the trees. As a young man I wanted the outsider's task, exile, and to find something beyond the village and be worshiped for the discovery. I probably gave Danny the idea of escape, we surely talked about it, but I never had the nerve to go, though I did manage a few years at university. I know dislocation is the great maker of selves. The attempt to tell stories has given me inklings.

Every story is beginningless and it's not necessary to know the end, just the meanders. Abi stands in a nine-month loop, between dark and first light, but I won't choose and order each moment. I have given up that kind of telling. Simply, I wait for backache to subside and hope Danny and Abi make a flammable thing and the next spark will burn us all up, not tear us apart. That is wishful.

4.

Abi meets Gee after school on the first day back. They stand in the dirt playground next to the swings. This is storm darkness at the end of summer.

"He is a bug," says Gee.

"James?"

"He is an insect."

"Why?"

"He's talking crazy. Like, he wants us to run away, and has no money and no idea of where to go or what to do. He wants me to go with him."

"Why? Has something happened?"

"What d'you mean?"

"Like, is something wrong?"

"He's just a bug."

❧

Tom's grapes took the prize every year, no beats missed, as his family grew, and his house was open each fall to a wide circle of cousins, friends, fellow growers, their envious faces flushed and astonished with that year's dark majestic wine.

I remember the windows and doors thrown wide to cloying fermenting fruit, children playing in and out of the deep yellow light, shouts as transient as quick bodies, and it all felt glorious and eternal. A full house, turbulent and joyful, never feels desolate. Our house, by contrast, has been dark with passing storms, gut-wrench thunder, increasing loneliness, when Annie died, when George went away, when we stood, cowed. Or is that how my memory shades it?

Low sun throws rippling shadows from the river across our rooms. Emma's touch everywhere.

∾

I don't know what the young campers are thinking, but they have infiltrated and contaminated us. Let me embroider the epoch. We are at the end of the familiar path. Long past the last frozen age and nearly at global cooking. Both poles, north and south, fill with life. Summer and winter bracket the story of stories. Ice sheets melting at an astounding rate. Thousand-mile tracts of silent taiga. Equatorial tribal wars. *The Beagle* was decommissioned and broken up and now the last pod of killer whales flows through a marine valley between islands. Danny lingers on the lane behind Abi's house; he sits his fuming horse and those islands fuss with clouds and lurid colour. Let them glow, our pillages, the forest raids, the shy ponies, our light-long thrusts clear of winter's invasive cells! Let them glow! We are whole and pristine the autumn we are nineteen and go to sea and discover our origin!

Four seasons. Four kids. Four suits to the deck. Four routes to the crossroad. Let's see how artfully we can carry the story between us, despite our own plights. My wife's knitting bones, my plans, your unknown participation. I must talk to Kata and Apocat, but tell them what? Ask them what?

"It's not that I begrudge you your work on that wall," says Emma, "but there are a thousand more important tasks."

∾

"It goes on as before."

"What does?"

"This."

"What?"

"Taste the air."

"What?"

"Smoke!"

"Ah. Fall."

"There's something else, Apo . . . "

Apocat shifts her buttocks into the dust between tree roots. "I'm listening."

Kata hisses. "Appetite. After nearly forty years."

Apocat sniffs the air. "Certainly. You are right. There's hunger."

"Something is on the way," says Kata. "What do you think?"

"I think you're right, love, but . . . I don't know. Sea? Pancakes? Sea?"

"Yes, yes. Something deep and rotten," says Kata. "Sulphurous."

"Is it winter coming?"

"I don't think so."

∽

All summer Apocat and Kata wove baskets by the river, day in day out. Every summer they weave baskets. Their baskets find their way into the houses. Every child in the village has slept in a river basket, opened its eyes to light through green curving reeds.

∽

Sunday, just into October, Danny was riding home. Tom walked out of the forest, strode stiffly toward him, lips moving.

Danny reined in.

"Trouble," Tom said. "Come."

Danny dismounted, let the reins dangle.

"A boy who works for me," said Tom. "Hanged himself."

∾

With what language can we approach this forest? It only exists now, as we enter the trees. Tom and Danny are not storytellers. They do not make meaning out of chaos. They tread together, grim, excited, into the story as if it doesn't exist, down the muddy path to the clearing where Danny climbs onto the stump and slits the rope with his knife. Tom catches the body and carries it to the lane. They lay James across the saddle and lead the horse to his parents' house. The house shambling, unsuspecting. Tether the horse. Tom carries the boy over the plank bridge, through the front door, and sets him on a couch. Danny follows, steps back when he sees the father, and watches. The father is still, and clearly in terror of the mother, whose voice from another room is asking, *Who is it?* James is pale and rain-wet. His black jeans and plaid shirt drip onto the couch, onto the floor.

Soon the father produces a bottle of red wine and the men drink and the mother crouches beside the boy, speaking under her breath. *My only one, my sweet boy, just raise your head and look at me, just raise your head and take a breath.*

What can I do? says the father. *Tell me what to do.*

His head swings back and forth, loose.

∾

The parents were blind with shock. All I can do is tell the story. I have my own as well as the village's to fit together, but to what purpose? How does obligation work? I know something of how they feel because Annie died, and even though no one listens and there's no true telling, I know that I'm obliged to try. Elders come to sit with the family around the fire, cards in hand, suits in order, red black red black, their eyes aglitter, while James reposes in the next room.

II

5.

Abi threw open the basement door and shook dust from her hair and sneezed. Behind her, Danny was sweeping around the trunks they'd just dragged to the middle of the cement floor, and his house was a mess, falling apart, windows cracked and dusty, and he hadn't spoken all morning. It was time to let the horses out. She crossed the flagstones and climbed over the low wall onto the dead thatch of summer's grass and headed down the path worn smooth by his family's years and years of to and fro. Down the hill to the horses shifting in their fixed-up barn that Danny called foursquare, tiptop, neat as a pin, and she loved because she'd known the place forever.

She paused at the door, listening, shivering. It was cold, below freezing maybe. Back at the house he was likely staring down at her. He knew, but not what he knew. He didn't know what she knew, but he knew. The horses inside were banging hooves on the ground, sensing her presence. Of course they didn't want to spend daytime shut in. She needed space to think. They needed morning light. She longed to run and run and run. There was such a difference between inside and outside, Danny's barn and the pasture, her house and the pass, life and death. Danny had told her about the wild ponies descended from domestic animals who escaped long ago to live in their valley for hundreds of years until recent summers when they'd crossed the plain looking for something. She fingered the barn wall, painted wood, once a tree. Everyone was trapped inside something. James had gone. What could she do? What were her choices? If she did nothing it would happen. What was inside would be outside. Red was in there. She had ridden him to the foothills, told him everything. She peeled a long strip of paint from the wall and took a breath and watched the crystals in the air as she breathed out and cradled her belly. She'd grown up riding her bike in and out the vine rows, the rows like waves interrupted, up and down the hills surrounding the cemetery where James was in the ground. She loved Danny's land because it resisted the vines; she loved to ride his land; she loved his beautiful barn, but not the ghost-house. Up there he was as restless as his horses down here, pushing furniture around, sorting boxes, throwing his stuff into the yard, piling it on his flatbed.

She followed the track around the worn timbers of the barn, scuffing her feet against clumps of stunted weeds, trying to remember what she'd decided in the night. About leaving, about talking to Danny. He'd do anything for her. If she did nothing, sooner or later her parents would know. Could he help? She blew on her fingers. Her legs were cold through her jeans and her jacket wouldn't zip up and she had on a thin shirt. Her mother was having a baby. Her sister had just had one. It was like a contagious disease. For fuck's sake. Fuck, fuck, fuck. She was changing but didn't know what she was changing into. Her baby was coming like a train.

∾

Half into the short bouncy ride to the dump, she swung to face Danny and said, "I'm pregnant," and he said nothing.

He swung the truck down the gravel road and parked and they got to work hauling out the boxes and bags, scaring up crows and a pair of ravens.

"Your parents know?"

"No. They don't even know I've had sex."

"Who else knows?"

"James knew."

"James."

"I'm not saying it's his or yours."

"It might be James?"

"I don't know."

"What are you going to do?"

"I don't know."

∾

An almost unwitnessed moment: dawn moonrise over the hills — all the vines picked clean leaving only the rows of *eiswein* grapes for the frost — and my old friend Danny out there riding the edge of the vineyard.

Danny and Abi. He should go back to the sea, west to his drowning.

I am avoiding doing something.

Which is what I have done my whole life — substituted stories, descriptions of the world, and a snail's eye view at that, for action. Fear, when all is said and done, is only a hand-written ticket, blurred and ratty, handed to the final captain, who has no time to punch it because the tide is turning. What do I do about Danny? Out there all is wonky horizon and a figure on horseback wandering away, irregular slant from the perpendicular, on a moonlit course. A speck in oil under a microscope.

∾

"Abi has a two-inch pussy," Gee said to Harry.

"Fuck off," said Abi.

"What?" said Harry.

"You know, a five-centimetre slit. Duh."

"Shut up," said Harry.

"Fuck off," Abi repeated.

"He's a shy boy," Gee said, "but you are my fond friend, my best friend."

"Leave her alone," said Harry.

They were in a steep lane between frosty hedges, going to the town dump, a place Abi had discovered yesterday with Danny. He called it the nuisance grounds. She'd been amazed it existed. It had been here all her life without her knowledge. It had been here, he said, since the town was founded. No one was supposed to use it any more, but they'd carted boxes of junk in his rusty old flatbed to the swamp anyway.

"It's true," said Gee. "Two inches. And she's scouting around for a boyfriend."

Abi turned and pushed Gee and Gee gave Harry a shove and he fell and dropped his .22. Gee stood over him, then made a face at Abi. "Such a fond friend you are."

"You're an airhead and a nincompoop," said Abi. "That's why nobody likes you."

"Bitch," said Gee. "Tramp."

"You are both crazy." Harry climbed to his feet and shouldered his gun. Mud on his rump and both knees.

"She doesn't like her pussy. You know why?"

"You are seriously unhinged," Harry said. "I'm not listening."

"James did it in there," said Gee.

They stopped at the gap in the hedge; there was a rough path through the black tree trunks.

"Yeah," said Harry.

Gee stepped onto the trail. "Let's go see. Let's go see the place, hey?" She wrapped her fingers around her own neck and made a throttled sound.

"Stop that," said Abi.

"Shut your mouth, Gee," said Harry. "James was our friend."

"Fire your gun, Mr Harry," Gee said. "Go on. One gun salute." She pointed into the trees.

They didn't go in, but kept on, past the mouth of the trail, down the lane until they could smell skunky water.

"There it is," said Abi. "There is the old dump."

Birch trees grew up through the skeletons of cars and trucks. The white trunks rose straight out of frozen pools pierced at intervals by tall spiky dead grass. A shadow from a single cloud drifted over the antiques drowning in iced-over water, the rusting hulks hanging like bones in the mist, while a line of splayed fence posts cut across to a little cliff where a pair of crows shrieked.

"Those are boxes Danny and me left yesterday," said Abi.

"What's in them?" said Harry.

"Who cares," said Gee. "It's spooky and it's freezing and it stinks."

They threw pebbles at the iron protruding from the swamp. Throwing stones to keep warm. Amid the clangs and splashes, they were all out of breath, Harry and Gee waiting for her to tell them why they'd come. The crows cawed from the branch of a ratty fir tree on the cliff.

"You don't know anything," Abi said.

"You think?" said Gee. "Think *I'm* stupid?"

"I know you are." She flicked the back of Gee's blonde head. "But I want to tell you. Both of you. You have to promise not to tell anyone else."

"Okay," said Harry.

"Gee?"

"If it's that you screwed James and that's what messed him up and that's why he killed himself, don't bother. I know that shit. Shoot a crow," she said. "Come on, Harry, shoot a mothershitting crow."

"Shut up," Harry said.

"I'm pregnant," Abi said.

"No way," said Harry.

"I was right!" said Gee. "I knew it!"

"No way," said Harry.

"Yes, I am."

"That fucking asshole," said Harry.

"It wasn't James."

"And then he strung himself up in a tree," said Gee.

"It wasn't James."

"Who then?"

"It doesn't matter."

"That's fucked," said Gee. "You're a total idiot. That old man?"

"No."

"Oh fuck," said Gee. "We're supposed to be your friends."

"You know it."

"What did you tell your parents?" said Harry.

6.

Danny rode home from the doctor's surgery past Tom's house, because of the girl. He often came this way after mass, after confession, the crossing spicy because Abi's mother Lucy had been in the church and Abi was inside the house, his mind slow afterwards with images of resurrection and longings and guilty shivers. Today as he took the alley behind the main street toward Tom's, the feeling gained in intensity. This was deep lust, more nuanced than mortality, and he welcomed it after the doctor's news. Despite what was going on inside his body, he felt fresher, freer, and younger than he'd felt in a long time. Years ago he'd had similar feelings for every village girl and some of the boys, but simpler. Death, complex and mysterious, was in a corner of his body, spreading, and every impulse in him was fleeing to this house of daughters, and one particularly beautiful girl. At twilight, the lane was a tunnel for the prevailing wind and a jubilant maelstrom of ragged leaves and thick white flakes. The house walls writhed with the family's wild indivisibility, at the centre of which was a well of clear water.

He shut his eyes and saw Abi.

Abi's baby swayed through his yawing thoughts, and some little ghost of himself was following, leaving the diagnosis behind, heading for the old seabed.

∾

Next day he spoke to the girl as she curried Red in the dim stable, shocked at how pale and thin her arms were in the rolled-up sleeves of her old plaid shirt. In tight jeans, her slender body leaning next to the horse verged on the impossible. Her round belly astonished him. He told her in short unconfident sentences that he would help in any way he could, she could ask him anything she wanted to ask, that he would help, not judge.

She kept silent.

"Up in the northern hills there's this valley," he said. "All summer there's wolverines, foxes, wolves, mountain cats, badgers and bears — and the ponies take to the slopes. You can camp up there the whole summer and never see a human soul."

"You've done that?"

"That was where I lived after I got home."

"From the sea?"

"Yeah. From the sea."

"I have never seen the sea."

∽

She had not. She saw it now through him; she saw sea, ponies, hills, the married woman, her infant girls, through him, as if he were a window or a door or hidden entrance. Somehow she had the key to that door or window or tunnel, and might one day, not now, discover rooms. Not today. This was enough — his voice, his eyes, the barn, Red's coat, all shining in a single burnished minute. The man, the night, stars through chinks in the boards. His voice, his eyes. Those waves. The sea.

Different, he said, from here, the rain like curtains at the start of a play. Like a bolt of cloth, he said, trees and rain and beach and waves. A single fabric. Green and wet.

She paused in her brushing to smile, to let him know she saw his kindness. The horse and man looking at her as if something else was going on. Something unavoidable, inevitable, but not at all graspable. Something from outside this moment. Danny said he had something to tell her. As he spoke, she heard the call of an owl. Beyond the man in the barn door, beyond the cold blue night. Steaming breath from the horses softened the timber edges and she and Red made a moon and one planet, the man a rough gate. He was pale. There were blue bags under his eyes. He was sick, might die. Was it time for her to go? And if so, where?

◦∾◦

Next day, she fixed breakfast for her sisters, made and packed her lunch and flew out the door, through the gate and across the plank over the ditch without a word to anyone. She didn't care what they thought they knew. Her sisters knew nothing. Whispers around school every day for a month. A fog of lies. They didn't know who she was.

Lovely little humped plank bridge. She felt sorry for its worn slippery boards. They creaked underfoot. Her father had built it a long time ago. There was ice down there in the stream, but the water went on underneath, flowing. Freezing cold, yet not frozen.

She passed nine wooden bridges on her way to Danny's. Four of the houses were empty. The stream in the ditch went on, always the same, but people were leaving and she was changing. She'd be fifteen next May. She'd have a baby. There was a new quietness in the fresh snow, a new whiteness. All night long storms had called above her attic room. She'd been nervous, especially through the long evening, and hadn't been able to keep still. "Got ants in your pants, fatty?" her sister's husband had teased her. Her sisters lying on the floor under blankets, drugged or hibernating. *It's snowing! It's snowing!* And she couldn't stop running to the window, running upstairs, running to the kitchen, and when their father brought smoky air in from the fields, she'd longed to follow the draft out to its source in the thickly falling snow. The house jostled by her father's passage had woken up. Peter had swaggered, bragged, her sisters had quit Crazy Eights and gone to the window.

Her body fizzed with danger. No one knew who she was. Nor did they know Uncle Danny, not the way she did. Last summer he'd begun to tell her his story. He'd told her about the landrace ponies, the small herd that still ran in the valley beyond the foothills, that no one else knew about. Last night he'd told her he might be dying, but not to tell anyone. He said her cells cantered unfenced, while his were trapped. *Landrace.* Her thoughts leapt in all directions. *Secrets.* What happened in Danny's cabin, Danny's barn, in the tent. Her dad was the only one who defended Danny. Her dad said Uncle Danny was a faithful person.

Nine bridges. Three times three is nine. Three men. Three possibilities. Lose the baby. Have the baby here. Have the baby somewhere else. Down the lane she was accompanied by kitchen sounds, until the village ended and the vine hills began. White hills combed by God into flowing lines, her mother said. An ice circle haloed the far-away sun. As she swung along the path curving up to Danny's house, she saw the ethnologist, his head down. He looked haunted, like a sleepwalker or a ghost. She let her hand brush the hedge: ice crystals sheathed tiny new buds.

∽

Standing at her bedroom window for hours as the days grew shorter, fingers against her belly, she tracked the line of white horizon hills left to right, right to left, as she counted her breaths. At each limit, set by the frame, she pushed her lower belly against the sill. To see how it felt. And listened to others in the house whose lives would be changed by her change. Maybe she wouldn't be able to carry the baby until it was ready for the world. Ran a finger, gathering a small dirt wave, through the grime on the windowsill and daubed her forehead. Looked for Double Mountain. She was so thin; the bump was a human person, already twitchy for something she probably hadn't got. Who to talk to? Had she told? In dreams, she had, and told and told and told, the telling dividing the village into those who avoided her and those who attacked her. If she wanted to take the focus off herself, she just had to name the person. That was no relief. Relief was to walk alone to the nuisance grounds. Relief was to hike the vine hills and imagine them waves, steady and repetitive, creasing the land. Snowy waves cresting. Below them iron plates floated over magma.

She would not be able to stay in the house much longer. Her mother would guess, her dad find out, and they'd send her away. She took good care not to show her belly, but her mother would guess anyway. Maybe Danny would let her fix up his parents' empty house and she could live there. No. She felt sick to her stomach, and that house was a nightmare and this house was a trap. Every day was a bit more horrible.

From her bedroom window on a clear morning like this she could see beyond the vine hills. She could see Double Mountain. Nothing was simple. Nothing would be simple again. She had told Danny, but not everything. The money he'd paid her for the summer's work would buy a train ticket to the city and a hotel. When it was time she'd go to a hospital. *Money, train ticket, hotel, hospital.* What was with these lists in her head? Who she'd tell, in what order; who would still like her, who hate her, who wouldn't care. Lists replaced every thought. Lists replaced hunger. At the end of lists, she'd be empty and have a baby, but then what? The horses in the barn were freer than she was. She'd told Gee and Harry and Emma, but not who. Emma would tell Charles and she didn't trust the storyteller.

ॐ

With her eyes closed, waiting for sleep, Abi listened to footsteps squeaking on the snowy lane and imagined men wading through drifts on their way to and from the centre of the village.

She lay between her sheets under the red blanket and surfed sleep, air huffing through the open window, footsteps loud then fading, guessing who, what direction, what purpose. Wild ponies trotted past, bone-cold snow in their faces, and she grew less sensible, and the ponies were a piece of childhood, inaccessible now, and she was a mare riding black wind, lungs aching, hearing only the drumming hooves and . . . She'd have a baby of her own. She'd have the baby in early May. Five months to go. Her mother would make a decision. Things would happen. Her father would banish her. Tall grass stung her legs as she flew through pitch-black meadows, nothing decided, for company the sleeping house, amplified and slowed down, the buzz of a plane passing over, the tidal moan of trucks on the highway. And then came Uncle Danny's footsteps, unmistakably slow, with a kind of swagger almost audible in the silence before each crunch.

She used to wonder when something would happen. Now it was happening. It was happening too fast. On her dresser were the castle and the dragon. Same dragon and castle as when she was tiny and ran up those microscopic white steps and along the battlement and into one of the doors to escape the dragon. Through the arched stone corridor to a miniature room carpeted and hung with rich fabrics, cushions everywhere, as if her home world did not exist, and all she had to think about was who to invite, be sure they did not bring sickness with them. Uncle Danny, of course. Her mother, no. Her father. But now the red dragon was dusty next to the useless castle, and no one would help her when the baby came. Her mother, no. Gee, no. Her sisters, no. Emma, perhaps. She got out of bed and went to the window. She ran her finger flat along the sill and gathered cool droplets. Emma could sleep in the chamber next to hers. Her finger was black from dirt from the wilds beyond the village. She traced the curve of her belly: this was her lowest rib, this her skin, elastic enough to stretch and hold a being. Marked a wet cross over her navel. What was it like in there? There was heartburn, ache, fear. There was a carpeted throne room hung with tapestries. There was her dream of her friends falling off the cliff. There was the urge to run downstairs to her bike and the fresh snow, to leave behind the castle and dragon. What was it really like in the throne room? Sanctum. Hidey-hole. What was there? A trove tree. A cupboard. Grail-box. Inside there was a child. (*Carry it to a real place, save its life.*) Don't worry. (*Get out.*) Not so worried. (*Get out!*) No, worried. (*For fuck's sake.*)

∾

Downstairs the house bristled, with all manner of furlings and unfurlings to do with rat catching, and Lucy and Abi sat together in the kitchen, their feet in a tub of steaming water, while men on ladders banged the house walls, and Tom and Peter hunted with dogs in the cellar.

"What will you do?" said Lucy.

"What?"

"Why not talk to Gee?" Her mother meant: Make it up, you need a girlfriend, not horses; you need to talk about James, not skip school and hole up. It's what they'd been talking about. It was a stupid idea. Her mother's belly was so big. She hated her questions. She didn't want to talk. She hated Gee. She would not answer.

Barking under the kitchen floor.

Their pink soft feet in the tub.

Ice inside the window glass.

Her mother was slow, so slow. She did everything slowly, child after child. Abi did not want her mother's astonished look. Her mother was mild, so mild and sympathetic. The whole house was freezing, waiting, and the rats were squealing, and babies were revolving in both their bellies. Her mother's baby would be a sister to hers — an aunt-sister.

"This refusal to talk is foolish, don't you think?" Lucy tried again. "What happened is terrible, but you are a good person. Gee is a good person. You had a fight, but you both are good."

Cold wind blew against the house and it creaked. They both looked toward the window. They heard the men's voices calling and Tom shouting back and the pounding on the walls intensified.

Danny had watched his boat sail away without him. She would run screaming out of the house with the rats, and quit the village — quit her mom, her dad, Harry, Gee, her sisters, all of them — even Danny, Mother Apocat, Mother Kata.

They would pull her back or try to; they'd break their necks to get her back.

Her mother's face was red from the hot oven.

A rat ran across the kitchen floor, another, a third.

7.

Lucy was big with her next girl, walking around the house with a half-full watering can, sprinkling the perimeter, protecting the house. The physical house and what was inside. The vase of grasses, the polished table, the old cat, the thready rug, blue wall plate, box of firewood, fire burning in the kitchen stove. Murky rooms were hard to fathom. East light in the window glass. She crossed herself. Her breath wouldn't melt the ice flowers on the glass. Indistinct shapes, blurred presences. Snow was falling cold on her head. She remembered when the house had first held Tom, when the first toddler had raced through doorways, room to room, to lodge crying between the man's legs, and him looking up, stupefied. The full ditch was frozen. And then she was nine years old, in another kitchen, her frostbitten feet in a basin of snow, learning where children came from, tears squeezing out of her eyes, her mother a ruddy bluster of soft cotton and electric fingers. *Here, Lucy, it will hurt but it will stop hurting. It will not hurt more than this.*

What was reaching out of this storm?

She waited in the snow like a bee outside her hive, worried about Abi. This daughter had grown quickly and bloomed early; soon she would vanish into the violent world and come back a stranger. *No wicked boy, no stranger, no wicked man, no stranger.* She continued her journey around the house, praying to winter, looking through the windows into the future just as *her* mother had circled her childhood house, the way her great grandmother had prayed around her own house ninety years ago, the way all the mothers had walked around a house in the darkest time, sprinkling water before it froze so living was safe. *No wicked boy, no stranger, no wicked man, no stranger.*

The windows spilled light onto snowfields.

The mother and her girls, the lioness and her cubs, the pride and the den. And she came around to the kitchen again, almost a lioness, shielding who she loved from the dilapidated shadows. *Listen.* Chaos locked in the ditch. Blood and thunder borrowed from the storm. And inside her was the last child stolen from such fluency.

She paused. What had her children not understood? There was her youngest daughter crawling across the tiles toward the sleeping cat, her small hands rising and falling. There's Abi, her next-to-eldest, staring out of the living room window, eyes big, long dark hair crazy, loose. Such pure white skin! No child was ever so wild and silent.

What must she tell them? She shook the last droplets from the brass rose, touched the spout to her lips, felt it stick. Her fingers frozen numb. *May no one fall out of this house.*

8.

On the wall in the barn was a blurred photograph of a boat with a black funnel and a mast in front and one behind. A little smoke came from the funnel. Danny had worked on the coastal freighter as a deck hand, a sailor.

In a stall was a horse dying.

The other horses as quiet as the faraway sea.

The orchard woman had taken the photograph; she'd aimed her camera from the gravel beach where she'd been walking her dog. With a queasy stomach he rose from the bench where he polished things to have a closer look at his life as it had been, as seen by the first woman he'd loved. She had become a set of stories, lost and then remembered. He felt seasick, looking at the boat. He had cancer. He would have the thing cut out. He knew where to find the dog on the stone beach — a brown blur bottom left of the photograph. When had he stopped seeing that dog? He studied the beach, mountains, boat. And it yielded. It was not only a sepia seascape in a dusty frame across from the stalls, hanging amid tackle, no longer the stain of something ancient and irrevocable.

He tapped the photograph with his fingernail. Coastal freighter steaming right to left. Perhaps he'd been at the helm; perhaps it had been his watch the day it was taken. That period had resurfaced in conversations with Abi. Nothing for years, and then the girl asking questions about his affair with the married woman. *Where was that woman now? Why hadn't they run away together? Had her marriage disintegrated? Had she left the pilot?* Abi's questions were a fresh link to the woman holding the camera. She had been thirty-three and he'd been nineteen. Now his eyes were seeing what hers had seen then. Was that possible, to look though the eyes of a girl at what he had once been to a woman? Was the purpose of love to cancel time? What was left of that young man?

∽

Love. Of course. He crossed to the big woodstove and opened the door and threw in a log. His bones felt tired. He slumped into the oak chair by the stove. Tortoise must feel like this. He looked at her where she lay, unable to rise, her ribs sticking out, her breath rattling, and felt tears coming. It took great effort to cross to her side and kneel. His fingers were frozen on her thick hide. He had always loved Tortoise, such a slow mare, and her eyes had looked at him, loved him slowly, for how many years? The account book of captures and births and deaths open to a day in the summer. Thirty years. Dust on the pages. The horse's life ending as the day outside was ending, freezing wind sweeping clouds away, whistling through gaps in the walls.

Day ended but he didn't want to leave her side until it was over, until she was dead. There was the sense of propriety, duty, faith, everything still to do. Food heavy in his belly, nausea. A pain in the ass. Likely he'd need the backhoe tomorrow. The living horses were rattled. The girl just left was still bright on that old kitchen chair in front of the feed chute, her ankles bare, her shoes immaterial things, beige, like dirty feet, her head cocked to one side looking at him tending the dying horse. The girl was not finished, not forgotten. Nor night. Nor fragrance. *The cattle are lowing, no crib for his bed.* Pity for Tortoise made him sob. He'd have to leave the horses. Of this life he would quit, he regretted the horses. *Loth to leave the horses.* Songs heard long ago. Rustle of hay. That kitchen chair and the oak chair brought down from the house winter before last.

Found my heart in the Bay of Biscay.

Chairs and framed photograph of the coastal steamer. He needed these items of his life, passed to him from experience or from his parents, and to fit them into the next cold day. It was none too easy, dying: dizziness, vomiting, weakness. For a man with no children death was a kind of blind from which to praise life, despite blood in the stool, red threads in Tortoise's snot. He felt so sorry for himself. Adjust your course every day, read tides, currents, season, angle of light, keep an eye on the old creaking chair by the stove, on the girl come loose from her family (she would never belong here), her squinting worried grey eyes leaping into his own because fifty-nine was too young to die. It couldn't be finished, couldn't be. What a giant bobbling squally thought! Such eyes! Such a winter!

"She won't be long," he'd said.

"What will you do?" she'd asked him.

"Borrow your dad's backhoe. Open the big doors. Tow her out."

"Can I come and help?"

"Sure, if you like."

Light cut across her midriff. Short fleece jacket, thin shirt, thin jeans, that prominent belly he'd been trying not to stare at.

"Aren't you cold?"

"Yes," with a shiver. "Not really." A smile. "Kind of. I'm okay. I like being cold."

It made him feel alive, careful. That she was young. That she didn't mind the cold. "Your parents know yet?"

She'd shaken her head. "No," with a smile. "Not exactly." A shiver. "Maybe. I don't think I'll come tomorrow. I don't want to see her — you know."

She'd shot out of her chair, out of the barn, and darkness had fallen, was still gathering. Through webby glass he could see his parents' rundown house (which was never his) up there on the hill. The one kitchen light, yellow, dim, muted as it flared through the hallway, the living room window, through cold shifting air down to his orbs hunting something. What? His thigh was cramping. He laid a hand on Tortoise's neck and a shudder rippled through his body. He stroked out her old legs. She was a foal again, just for a moment.

∽

Someone.

The useless. The eavesdropper. The tattletale. The betrayer. The failure. The condemned. The guilty. Him. *You. It's you.*

Who woke and rubbed his eyes, asked as usual no question. Simply stood from his cot there in the barn. The stove still warm. On the straw Tortoise was awake. Alive, but barely. The other horses' ears aswivel. All breathing silence. A visitor. A meeting.

"Your name is Harry."

"Yes."

"She's not here."

"I know."

"You should be home."

"I wanted to talk to you."

"Go home, I'm busy with a horse."

"I heard you were sick."

"Who told you that?"

"Kata." The boy wouldn't meet his eye, was as restless as he was tired. "How are you doing?"

"Like shit." He stifled the urge to talk about that moment in the doctor's office when something inconceivable was known, or disclose the diagnosis, the order of coming events, the prognosis. It was not right. Not with this boy. Not Harry. He waved his arm. "What do you want, then?"

"Did you and Abi . . . "

"No, we didn't."

∾

Danny and Tom picked their way up the frozen path, ice crystals scattering, half moon above. They went single file, not talking. Only their laboured breath signalled their passage up to the house.

"Thanks for the help," Danny said.

Once inside the house, Tom shouted how cold the place was. "Don't you keep a fire burning?"

"I don't live here."

"You're living in the barn."

"That's right."

"Why leave the lights on?"

Danny shrugged. He felt the dismantling loneliness of the rooms. He felt thin in his gut and went about the ritual of sticks and paper spills and threw a match in. "Be warm enough soon. Have a seat."

Words might later be erased. Welcomes erased. The conversation about to launch itself deleted. He hadn't wanted Tom in the barn, but he'd needed his help to move the horse. He put the kettle on the stove and opened the grate.

"You know, then?" Danny said.

"About Abi?" said Tom.

"Yes."

Tom rubbed his hands together. "She won't talk. She's with you a lot."

"Oh yes."

"She talk to you?"

"She chatters a bit when she's happy."

"You know what I mean."

"Yeah. She tells me a bit."

"You know who it was?"

"No."

"Looks like you're packing."

"Just turfing the old stuff out. Eliminating, getting shut of."

"Abi's still useful with the horses, then?"

"That okay with you?"

"It's okay." ·

"She loves the horses."

Danny poured water over the tea bags in the cups and sat down across from Tom at the table his father had built. He felt his muscles aching. He was exhausted. Towing the horse, digging the shallow hole, burying the horse, the uphill walk from the barn to the house, grape hills rising and falling — these repeated, the buckets of earth repeated, the paths multiplying.

His toward uncertain health. After the operation, they wanted to hook him up to a bag and push chemicals into him that would make his hair fall out and his teeth loose in his head. Fuck that. It had taken a year to straighten and shore up the old barn, replace the split boards, double up the old studs, re-shingle the roof, fashion a new door, new windows, install the stove. It still wanted painting but he'd run out of time. He'd worked every day for a season, and returned every night tired and happy to his old room and sleep. His parents' house had been all right then, and it was close to the work. His cabin on the bench had been neglected, too far from his horses, the barn work. He hadn't gone camping all summer, hadn't visited the valley. He'd thought the ponies all caught or gone, but one day in the fall he'd seen a small herd with foals in the distance: life in the valley had gone on unobserved during his frenzy of renovation.

"Lucy wondered — I'm supposed to ask you to come for Christmas Eve," said Tom.

"I'll be there."

"You look like hell. Are you all right?"

"That appaloosa cross was a wonderful horse."

"Yeah. I'm sorry. What's going on, Danny?"

"Nothing, Tom. Abi's a gentle girl. The horses were apprehensive about her, but she's got the touch. Looking after them does her good."

"I'm not talking about the damned horses, Danny," said Tom.

~ 155 ~

This old fixed-up barn. The dividers horse-bitten. Sheaffer's stall cracked through to Tortoise's. Tooth marks of dead horses. Some of the landrace were ghosts before they decided to be captives again. He made hot chocolate on the primus.

Harry came looking for you.

Your dad was here.

The unspoken words hung like straw dust in needles of sun.

"You are such a beautiful girl," he said. "You look seasonless."

"What does that mean?"

"Not young, not old. Out of this world."

"Why did Tortoise die?"

"Want of breath."

She glared at him. "I'm serious."

He nodded slowly. "Something in her gut."

"She was old."

"No she wasn't."

They had nothing to talk about except horses and the sea. Tell me again the story of the ponies. Why did you catch them? Which horse what year? What is it like to be at sea? What is it like in a storm? Never: *When will you die? Who is the father?*

9.

"Red's a big horse," Danny said to Tom, but your girl's capable.

We were all gathered at Tom and Lucy's house for Christmas Eve. I looked round the table as Tom uncorked the wine, poured out seven glasses. For Jane and Abi, the eldest of their five daughters, for Peter the son in law, for Danny, for my wife, myself, himself. Lucy held her hand over her glass.

"Subtle, Tom," Emma said after a sip. "Hint of peach?"

"Happy Christmas," said Tom, raising his glass.

"To James's family," said Lucy. "We are avoiding that. That is what we're avoiding."

Out the window snow swarmed around the single yard light. The conversation had been about motherhood and children, then horses, riding, the wine, and now turned to the dead boy. The giggling twins would not heed their mother's call for silence. I could see what we were avoiding. James was in the room, the too-hot room, and Lucy was staring at Abi. Abi was looking at Danny. And Danny had looked too much at Abi. That circuit was the problem. Then it was quiet and we were all waiting, poised.

What was barely felt: a thickening of blood in the thighs, expanding time and puzzlement, faint roiling in the gut.

Lucy, the ever-pregnant mother, was avoiding her husband's eyes, while he, stubbly and wide, gulped his wine, and the twins continued their private game that involved glances and giggles and blushing. Danny had stopped eating.

"Are you all right, Danny?" Lucy said. "Your hands are all red. Your eyes are bloodshot."

Danny held up his bright hands. He was ruddy as a fall leaf. To see him was a shock. He wore a dark leather jacket and a white shirt and a thick gold chain, but his face was beetroot and tears were rolling down his cheeks. He lifted his head and stared at us, then held up his rough spotted red hands. It looked as if he might faint, might vomit.

"It's true," Tom said. "Your face is red, Dan."

Danny said, "I have to move to the city to see to a tumour."

Above the table drifted a haze of heat. The shadows stirred, furring the edges of things. He held up his hands. Emma was bent forward in concern. Lucy and Tom were giving Danny all their attention, but no one could help him. I could see that. No one could give him what he wanted.

"What tumour?" said Emma.

"Bowel."

"Your eyes," Abi said. "Your eyes are so bloodshot."

"Ah," he said. "It's too hot in here. The room is too hot."

"Is it bad?" said Tom.

"Is there a good cancer?"

"You should lie down before mass," said Lucy.

"I'll be all right. I don't think I'll go to mass."

"Red," the children repeated. "Red. Red. Red. Red."

∽

Each moment. The next moment. She should not draw attention to herself; if she says nothing this will lead to no attention; although she likes his attention, she doesn't want this attention; he's staring and staring. Her mother is staring, too. Her dad and sisters and Peter and Emma and Charles go on with their stew, why couldn't Danny and her mother?

Her dad says, "You're getting surgery, then?"

"Don't know. Radiation first, then back here for a while, I guess."

Then Peter, mouth full of meat, is talking about the snow, the frozen earth, the vine roots. Her dad tells the story again of cutting James down and carrying him home and how he looked lying on the couch. *Poor James. Poor family. Poor Gee.*

And that's the end of conversation.

Everything's quiet except for spoons in bowls and her niece sucking her sister's nipple in plain view of everyone and Uncle Danny red as a devil. She feels hot herself, a red heat rising from the middle of her chest. The plague has jumped from the tiny castle right into her own house, and she can feel it flooding her neck and face. James hanged himself in the woods because he had the red death and even though the members of her family are not lords and ladies painted and dressed up, they will contract the red death. Her sisters and father will get it; Peter and Charles sipping from their wine and giving her the evil eye already have it: she can smell death on them, see it in their faces. Tortoise died of it. Uncle Danny's so red she can't take her eyes off him. Her mother is catching it right now. Perhaps only Emma is immune — she looks cool, calm.

"Are you all right, Abi?" her father asks.

She tries to rise, her chair legs moaning on the wood floor, but before she can escape, Uncle Danny takes a long look into her eyes, pushes up from the table, and totters to the ottoman. "Go on with your dinner," he says. "I'll be fine in a minute."

All of them know or will soon know.

Dinner continues around the table as if all is hunky dory, James gone without a trace after hanging from a tree, Uncle Danny helping her dad cut him down. But nothing is hunky dory. A baby stirs in her belly. A baby stirs in her mother's belly. Her niece is drinking red wine from her sister's nipple. Red death stalks the house.

∽

The girl poised, spoon aloft, her slight neck bent, face turned toward her mother. The pale mother receiving the look. The living man shivering on the brocade ottoman next to the standard lamp. The girl getting up from the table, crossing the room to kneel at his side.

∽

Uncle Danny smiles. "I'm so sorry."

She nods. This is death. Cold and red-handed. This man she knows. She touches his red fingers. They are cold.

A pass high in the northern hills. A single tree. Her scalp cooled by a drip falling from a new leaf, burst of red behind her eyes. Young men and women of distant cities filing through her, through the pass: new families to replace the boring people at the dining table.

Baby Sophie leans back and gurgles, then hunts and catches Jane's nipple. An invisible stream passes from Jane's body into Sophie's mouth. Something tangible passed from men's bodies into hers last summer. Something visible will pass from her body into her family. They don't know what she is capable of, what she has done. She's trapped in this house at Christmas watching Sophie's lips tug at the fat nipple while a cousin baby sleeps in her belly. Uncle Danny showed her the cabin; she showed James.

She looks down at the gaunt shape on the ottoman, his face like a pomegranate, purple rings under his closed eyes, his sticky lips moving and dim thoughts, not flesh at all, surface: horses from the sea, boys from men; the baby in her belly, hardly flesh at all, has thoughts that already double her life. Pregnant mares accompany her the way the water in the ditch creeps round the house, and she wants to flow too, in the company of wild ponies, past the houses, through the village, over the vineyards to the open land, through mountains to the sea. They are all she can attend to, these ponies. And while she attends, she looks down at her worn slippers. Her toes are in there, small, straight, white toes, and if she stood they'd take root or give her purchase and traction. There is the choice to stay or go. She regards the men. They are so simple. Uncle Danny really gave her Red and has promised her all his horses. What can a girl do with a barn full of horses? Gee asked. James said he's not worth studying, that old man. She feels the slow return of the present as the dishes are cleared from the table and tries to imagine the young guy Danny was, but she's just mixing him up with James who has hanged himself in the woods.

∽

Danny limps with Abi's help over the icy silver planks to his truck. With his arm around her, he feels ancient, or alien. Tom's house looks just plain alien. What the hell. He sits behind the wheel with the engine running, while she crosses back and turns at the gate to wave. A tide of nausea. Has he touched her? Has he leaned on her? He lights a joint. She has promised to come tomorrow. She will tend the horses while he's away. Cancer, cancer, cancer, cancer. If he says it enough times will it feel his gaze and retreat? He will need to confess but what more can he do? They need company, the horses, need grooming and moving out to pasture on warm days, in for the night, food and water, for as long as they live. She loves them but is too young, and she has a wild streak. She reminds them of freedom. He rolls down the window and leans out. "You can manage the horses?"

She says yes. She knows what to do when it freezes.

He says he'll pay her in advance. "Can you come tomorrow?"

She says sure.

"Come early. Want to go to the cabin one last time?"

She stands at the open gate and shrugs, then closes it behind her and walks toward the house. He winks his lights. He sits in the truck and floats with his ghost parents off to Florida — there they are, highballs in hand, two blurred, epic, flapping unravelled stories, bowels married in Celtic knots. That he should face this now. Radiation, surgery. Knots in his own twisted tale. Six weeks to burn the sucker down to size. But at least. At least what? He sits in his truck and flicks away the roach, checks the rear-view — grey puffing smoke, exhaust — and is transported to the alpine pass high in the northern hills, his forehead cooled by a drip falling from a leaf, burst pollen on his fingers. He doesn't want to die, nor does he want to be surrounded by strangers in a city hospital. Above all he wants to avoid being summoned by Tom and Lucy. He would rather ride into the mountains and have Abi attend to his passing, Abi and the horses. If he knew for sure he was dying, he'd take the horses up there and start a new landrace, make camp and let her witness what he really was.

10.

"Has to be we're travelling, not the mountains," said Danny, "but I like to think they are moving on us."

"Yeah," said Abi.

"Noticed it the first time I ever rode out here and I always look for it. It's striking when there's fresh snow on the slopes. I figure it must affect the horses when they run, but I guess they're at home with such confusions. Figure and ground. You know what I'm saying?"

"Yeah. We studied it in Art."

"Did you?"

"Where's the pass?"

He pointed. "See the reserve?"

"Yeah."

"It's right there, between those two cliffs. That dark slash?"

They were walking out into the plain on Christmas day, Danny on Solomon and Abi on Red, and bells were ringing from the village behind them. Time sticks. Ahead were the mountains, too young to know they were once molten. To each side the lowering sky. Light was flat, grey. They'd left at dawn, galloped to warm up as soon as they could make out the strewn rocks. Now the sun was rising, hooves and breath were the only sounds and every time Red snorted, Solomon snorted. And when Red shook his head, Solomon did the same.

"Solomon's just a copycat," said Abi.

Danny laughed.

"Where'd you get that name? Paraclete."

"It's Greek, Abigail. Close helper. When there's misery in human affairs Paraclete will advance you a notch toward spring."

"He loved Tortoise."

"Yes he did."

"Is he mourning?"

∾

Abi looked where Danny was pointing, at the two pony-and-rider shadows made long by the early sun. The mountains did seem close; they were nearer than she'd ever seen them. They looked completely wild. Unrelated to her in any way. *Advance me,* she whispered, and squinted at the black slash above the distant hills, trying to understand this package of shadows and sky and mountains inside her. Something was building; it was how much Danny loved her; how much he loved the horses, how close she was to figuring everything out. What was going on inside her could find meaning in Danny's words, the way it already had in his speaking; ever since he'd told her of the ocean and the waves, she'd felt them in her; she was a kind of wild horse. She was sure that was it. And he was what an adult could be near the end of words.

"Desire was the foal of Paraclete. Paraclete was the foal of Mimesis. Mimesis was the foal of Longing."

She didn't know how the names had bubbled up through Danny, the ordinary and the magical. While he dismounted to pee, she asked Red what she should do, her voice a skinny knife in the sparkling air, then turned to the village behind her, river lost in its channel carved by an oldness she could feel in her bones, and waited for the answer. Red shivered, then shook his head, mane spinning out a rainbow, and they completed a circle, the horse dancing as if to prepare a direction, new possibilities appearing and disappearing in the muscles flexing beneath his hide, in the complications his legs spun him through, joints performing copies of fellow joints, hoof echoing hoof, fetlock answer to fetlock question.

"Danny, are you going to die?" she called.

"Yes." He climbed back into his saddle.

"Why didn't you leave them wild?"

"They were going to fade out. There were fewer births every year. Each spring they came back from the mountains thinner and fewer. This is what we do with our lives."

∽

They rode to the foothills, then it got stormy and Danny said they'd have to spend the night in the cabin. The day was dark when they got there. They settled the horses in a lean-to full of hay, then went into the single webby room. He still wore the gold chain under his leather jacket that flashed in the gloom as he gathered kindling from cardboard boxes ranged along the walls.

"I'll have to stay up to keep the fire going," he said.

She blew into the hot chocolate and listened to him talk, drifting in and out of sleep, her body still swaying with the motion of the horse, until the blanket fell from her shoulders and he was lifting her into a cot in a recess beside the stove.

All night, Danny was up in the loft talking.

He'd discovered the pass thirty-five years ago during an early spring camping trip to the basin-land north of the reserve where he'd watched the wild herd for a week and one day just before sunset, after a day of exploration and rain showers, he'd isolated his first pony in a meadow between two hills — a small filly, restive, nervous, regal — surprisingly easy to cut from her sisters. She'd stood in the scrub and watched his approach, nickering, let him lay his hand on her flank. He'd kneeled at her side and stroked her, finding a wound, once deep but almost closed now, on the inner thigh of her back right leg. When he rode off again she followed, and the others kept pace at a distance. A rainbow spanned the valley and they flew under its arc toward the mountains and reached the pass just ahead of the first stars.

Then Abi was talking, everything flowing out of her, everything she'd said and not said to her family, to the villagers; when she slept she dreamed of them all gathered on a grassy slope by the sea.

She watched the gold flash in the first light as Danny descended the ladder from the loft and got the stove roaring and put the heel of whisky (his indulgence, he called it) away in a high cupboard, and took from an adjacent cupboard a tin of coffee and filled a pot with water, set the pot on the stove. She sat up and tucked her feet under her and pulled the red blanket closed in front. She felt like an old woman, tired and scraggly, her face greasy, new pimples starting. Everything seemed lurid as day came on and all she wanted to do was lie down again and sleep. Just shut her eyes and disappear.

"Every day for a few hours, give or take," Danny said. "Course, you don't have to. I don't expect it from a girl with your troubles."

"I don't mind," she said.

"You might later."

"Are you scared of dying?" she said.

"What I'm scared of is hospitals," he said. "And I don't want to leave here. Whatever comes back won't be me."

"If you don't come back, I can't keep looking after them."

"I know. There's your dad or Charles, and what about Harry? They would help out."

"I can't wait to leave," she said. "I can't wait to get out. It's like the longer I stay, the more there is to lose. I keep having this dream of a white ship as big as a mountain, and it can sail on land and just wipes out everything, the whole village, just when I have something to say and everybody's listening, and I can never get the words out. I always wake up crying."

ॐ

On their way home he rode ahead. Abi stared at his white hat with its black band, his hair a grey bush under the brim. His thin sunburned grimy neck, the frayed white shirt collar. She watched him gallop a ways, then stop. He stood in the stirrups, gazing back at her, or at the way they'd come. In the familiar landscape, he seemed like a prince disappointed in his father's kingdom. The flatland was like the sea that had once covered it and the vine hills where they lived were like islands, still a long way off. This was their last ride. Soon she'd be alone with the horses. She closed her eyes and let Red walk on and willed the white ship to appear, now, on the horizon, like a hundred-mile wall; and she and Danny would marvel and look at each other. The towering steel would wipe them out in a flurry of tumbling rocks and vines and bricks and debris, and she would see the world for a second as it was, wide and conscious and beautiful. She would feel no guilt. Her family at the breakfast table, councillors at the council table, birds on the ground — all swept away.

When she opened her eyes, Danny was regarding her.

"What's up?" he said.

"Is there ever a time when nothing is happening and nothing's about to happen?"

11.

July, I know. It began in July. July. Cauldron hot.

The cells dividing. Some right, some wrong.

∾

I take Polly along the ice-fringed river. As usual, we meet the black dog with three legs. Apocat and Kata sit wreathed in smoke, bundled in blankets on the porch of their house. I flap my arm at them. They don't register my presence. I am no less lonely, no less impatient, than I was last summer. I tell Polly that the months slip and slide while the seasons follow their course, with the usual traffic, and it's nothing that hasn't happened before.

Although instincts have lost their way and smokers on their porch won't diagnose or solve the village's ailment, my wife's arm is mending. Every night, woken by her pain, I go out onto my sheltered promontory and sit with candle, glass of wine, shivering at my desk. *What of Abi's pregnancy? She was drunk. She got drunk with Danny. What have they done? What will they do next? Papagana. Pabbivinnar. Ayabmenang. Apanyer. Vatergewinnt. Babamafanikio.*

On the hanging path, Polly at heel, I hear voices from the nuisance grounds and set off through the trees to the gully. On the shore of that intoxicated sea are two kids throwing pebbles at an engine projecting from the swamp. I recognise Gee and Harry. From the shaggy cutbank a family of crows caws down.

Almost home, a movement in the fence shadows catches my eye. The black dog with three legs stands his ground. Polly growls.

I crouch in the shelter of my wall in the afternoon under winter's monumental blues. Our village is slipping. True. A consortium has been buying us out, house by house, farm by farm, for a decade. They plan a super quarry to the north, and say our town is perfect for housing and offices, a staging ground for operations. How big? Big. For what? For aggregate. To surface-mine aggregate. What does this mean? That the vineyards will disappear. Massive wheeled hoppers, crushers and washers will dominate the landscape. We'll make money and retire into memory, loss of memory. Where we move to, what will happen to Danny and Abi, will matter less and less then not at all. Consortium. Conglomerate. Aggregate. Emma is organizing a petition against the developers; a research committee has been struck, and a committee to build a website and get the word out. We are organizing a series of town hall meetings for the spring. But don't we need new families?

I pat my pockets and look out. Last July I sat in this spot watching Danny's horses crop the curly grass below the vine hills. Apocat and Kata sat near the river, under the big tree, in a haze of dust kicked up by the rain, weaving their lazy baskets. Was I as worried then as I am now? We were all younger then.

Fine snow crystals land on my knees.

The rest of the villagers will be sitting in front of their fires, the year's work done, all the merchandising and maintenance, and the girl's pregnancy and the boy's death no longer stir the bare branches, and mention of Danny's illness won't even change the light. Even though there are no wild horses, and machines fly overhead, the people will still doze before their dying fires every winter afternoon. The village has thrived through wars and complicated migrations and our neighbours' worry and envy and confusion. We kept our noses to the ground. When the fires go out there's the sound of laughter, hooves, then stillness and night.

∾

One windy January morning we met at the river to say goodbye to Danny. We were a small group waiting under the big tree, all of us freezing by the time he appeared leading three horses. He looked miserable. He stroked the face of each horse. He kissed Lucy and Abi, shook Tom's hand, hugged Emma and bowed to me.

"Last time you left," I said, "we were both young and did not say goodbye."

Kata and Apocat appeared trundling downhill between two mounds of snow-covered vines, sun surging behind them.

"We had to see you," Kata said, "before you ran off."

Danny hugged her. Apocat smiled and drew her shawl tight. To the east boiled the sun, a wild anxious balloon, and the horses whinnied and nickered and stamped in the gusting wind, and Abi took their reins and led them back up the path while Tom and I kept Danny company to the edge of the cultivated hills and along the river.

At the Greyhound stop beside the bridge Tom ranted about the quarriers' plans to build new roads and a subdivision.

Danny lit a joint. "That's not news to me." He staggered, coughing, then gripped my shoulder. "I have told Abi she can depend on you and Emma." He turned to Tom. "We all know the land out there is useless for agriculture and pasture."

Tom said: "*They* do not know shit."

We stood, breaths crystalizing, and watched the river; the edges were frozen and in the middle eddies spun debris; the surface purled and settled into a gold sheet in the early sun.

III

12.

So Danny has left for his essence of sun, and a consortium is buying up its last puzzle pieces. I cannot say how much my own processes have coloured things (I am suffering — gastritis, the doctor thinks, and acid reflux, as well as the back agony), but the present isn't all my own doing, obviously. Last summer's visiting kid-scientists, staring at their screens more than at us, have tapped change's hieroglyphics on the sunny field, on the village green. To what purpose remains to be seen. I knew their parents' generation; I do not know them. A few years ago I watched Abi, Gee, Harry and James play together in the glass room I built for our school. As ten-year-olds, James and Gee were loud show-offs, while Abi and Harry were sober, inquisitive, introspective, and they listened. Emma fed the kids lunch and nursed them when they were sick. Indeed, I've spent more time watching children than tracking any other fauna or flora and have discovered one thing: Comes a time when children outgrow their parents' stories and want only the ones they tell themselves; with the great sagas of their lives yet to be lived, they invent the world. Loud, ill-mannered, selfish, pimply, cruel, passionate, thoughtless, clumsy, forgetful, lazy, sleepy, deaf, obsessive, they burst from their families like shooting stars and found their own versions of life on what appears to them to be an uninhabited rock. I have had life enough to observe some of these aliens all grown up, quietly kind, magnificent, serious, attentive and thoughtfully in train to their own offspring that look to me now like dots crawling in circles.

My own kids seemed miraculously potent, then turned impenetrable. What Danny sees in Abi, I saw and see: her quick body, her wise grace. What he is to her, I could not say. I cannot say.

Emma challenges me to the bone, for which I am grateful. Yesterday we fought about Danny until she held her arm in the air, which reminded me we are still vulnerable. She got drunk with Danny. They rode off north for a lesson in July, the heart of summer. North with a couple of litres of wine and she fell from her mount. Wine at his cabin; the fall on the way home. Danny did not get her to the clinic before she passed out, and the doctor was not due for a day, so she was airlifted to the hospital. I was terrified that she'd broken her back. This lesson, adventure, mishap, way-point, had all the earmarks and half-imaginings of an affair — they'd ridden off my map and it felt as if we'd been preparing for this, the three of us, for a long time, and it was the precursor of some radical conversion.

ॐ

She thinks I'm avoiding her when I'm labouring outside, long hours on the wall days it's warm enough, until I'm in darkness, fitting the stones by touch alone, the brandy bottle leaning in its purpose-built niche.

Actually, dear earthworms and children, it's my creator consciousness, undifferentiated, what's behind all voyages, homecomings, that is burrowing deeper into the work.

"Look," I say to her when she joins me at dusk. "These rocks are pure matter for change to write its signs on."

"It's bitter, that wind. Will you come inside?" She is wrapped in a big padded coat, her face pale.

"Can you tell me exactly what happened out there with Danny?" And I fit another stone in place.

She gives a snort. "All summer you were either out here or following the children or talking to that tent couple . . . Will you come inside? We need to talk about these mining people."

"In a minute."

"Charles, it just happened. I fell off my horse. It just happened. Look at me. You have your head down all the time."

"I know. It's true."

"How do you see the rest of our lives together?"

"Peaceful, I hope."

She stands shivering and I want to leap the wall and take her in my arms but don't.

"Charles, what is it? What do I have to do?"

∾

She can't knit because of her arm. I should help her on with her shirt. She winces. Her pain's a grating thing, terrible to witness. Her voice is compressed by it.

∾

Emma and I were drawn into the Home School idea when Annie died. We pulled down the west wall and built a glass extension and bought curtains and cushions and mats and soft balls of all sizes. Emma organized and supervised work and play. I taught science and art and told stories.

Abi, Harry, James and Gee, the last of our kids, came to us when they were about six. Her first day, Abi smuggled herself through the crush of other children and slipped out of the window into the garden, jumped on her bike and was gone. Next day, she would not come inside. She was fierce and headstrong and wouldn't sit with the others for weeks. Of course she reminded me of Annie. When at last she came into the glass room, she stayed beside the open door. I have never met any person so lost to rain or wind, some twirling, flitting or sleeping detail.

Each year there were fewer students, parents preferring the exuberant village school, but we kept things going for eighteen years, until there were no kids left under twelve.

∽

Third brandy by the wall. Mid-afternoon, late winter. *We are a gentle people, used to easy laughter. A hundred years ago when we were young . . .* What should come next? I'm not sure whether I'm having trouble with memory or trouble with time. Where is my glove? Accidental displacements seem more imperative than consortiums and potential mining concerns. I keep losing work gloves, for instance. Though I have always lost gloves. My mother was always admonishing me for losing a glove. I begin with two gloves, then there is one. I'm in one time, then another. At the centre of my expanding orbit is the other glove, the lost glove opposite to the one I have that proves there once were two, hugging my fingers out there at the end of my arms, flapping or pointing. Alley-oop! Non-locality. And then a new pair.

I need both my work gloves because the rocks are rough. Leather, with well-stitched seams. Gloves help the work and work makes the man.

The three kids passed the house early this morning, going toward the dump. They were insubstantial through the wobbly window glass: Abi serious, Gee taunting, the tall boy Harry aloof. Reunited, I guess. It's not that I don't care about politics and the future of the village, it's just that the wall and gloves and the comings and goings of these young people fascinate me more. I opened the door to a few spring birds already singing madly and greeted the kids. They were not gentle, they were full of harsh laughter. *They come to us, we don't control them, and in their presence we are not so sure of ourselves, of who we are, not so free.*

Emma knows my obsessions, of course she does. She sees through my notebooks, my wall, my visits to the river and the dump. She thinks the wall interesting but too much, too long. *When will it turn?* she wants to know. *What are you dividing? You will run out of land*, she says. I tell her it doesn't want to turn. It wants to go on and on. *Well it can't*, she says. *And neither can you.* That's why I've started the sandy path. *And then what?* she asks. Oh, then we'll find out. Alley-oop! Two points and a line.

Getting lost, losing place, being wily, using cunning, getting away from family, finding truth. I don't know how to engage it all, but when I praise this wall, lay my palm on frozen stone on an afternoon like this — *crows marking the day, crows guarding the nuisance grounds with its castoff belongings and secrets* — I feel life spinning around me and know what I am.

I have seen the sea, had dreams of storms, smelled the tide when Danny told his stories. If he so loved the sea, why didn't he ever go back? The horses he captured kept him here. The ponies gone wild, brought home, adapted and bred once more to stable and pasture — he accomplished that. A wall that doesn't end cannot contain anything. An incomplete and temporary division at best, as Emma would point out if she wanted to bring in her Noah or Job. She thinks I live in a state of doubt. And yet she's kind and patient, even with her broken arm, and she only half-turns her face away when I question her faith.

This morning at breakfast she told me how self-centred, how self-absorbed I am becoming.

"Yes I know," I said.

"You never listen. You will not meet me here." She touched her chest. "I want a real conversation."

"Self-absorption keeps me at my task."

"You take pleasure in nothing but yourself."

"I'm at least a puzzle, right? Fascinating, right?" I said.

Our breakfast almost finished, I looked out of the window and saw the kids passing, opened the door to birds, etcetera. Time and place and walls and hills were scrims and backdrops.

"What are we going to do?" said Emma.

"In so far as I'm part of this?"

"What?"

"Part of all this down here, with God up there?"

She made her annoyed clicking sound. "Did you talk to Apocat and Kata about the consortium?"

"No. I forgot."

"You will?"

"Yes."

"We have to bring the band on board."

"We will, Emma."

"And ask them about Abi."

Polly scratched at the door to be let out. Good Polly. I got up and let us both out. This little dog knows the truth. Truth is, we need to sniff the ten thousand things. I need brandy in the morning, at noon, at five, and Polly needs to walk down the road away from home along a brightening lane through melting snow. Let responsibility drift. We need time free, to be answerable to no tradition, no conception. Polly needs to mark her boundaries. I need to study the crumbling roadbed that once led whole and true to Emma; her arm is mending; I think she is telling me something like this: fix yourself or else. The *else* is the starlings in formation, the long line of family — a little diminishing tribe, tinier and tinier in the past or future.

∾

Emma doesn't trust me, but I don't mind that. I won't tell lies. Stories are not lies. I slip the brandy from its little cave and tuck it inside my jacket, then go down the road to drink with Apocat and Kata in their neat, ramshackle bungalow. I ask what I intended to ask; what they say isn't useful. Here is the gist, here are the bones.

13.

The weavers watch me pour golden liquid from the bottle into teacups, then sip, sip, take turns to name smells from the village that apparently waft in through their open kitchen window.

Kata throws cardboard into the stove. "Consortium," she sneers. "What do outsiders always want, Charles?"

"Land," I say.

Apocat rocks on her heels. "It is a very cloudy day," she says. "Boy, it is just one big cloud up there."

"Pay attention, Apocat," says Kata. She turns to me. "She is gathering herself."

"A little more brandy, perhaps?" Apocat muses.

"Can't dance without music," says Kata.

I pour. We drink. They tell me to feed the stove. They tell me to smoke.

"Your friend, Danny," says Apocat, "needs to keep his life a bit longer."

"Will he?" I ask.

"Danny has an appetite," she says. "There's no better point in any contraption. Look at that red glow. A man is ill. A boy is dead. A girl is pregnant."

"What about the girl?" I ask. "What about Abi?"

"Animals are at the end and beginning of everything," says Apocat. "Look at that red cloud. All that lonely mess."

"So what do I tell Emma?" I ask.

"You say to her these strangers want the land," says Kata. She touches her sister's knee. "But why do they, Apo?"

"Just like you people, they want to control the future," says Apocat.

"How do we fight them?" I ask.

Apocat still is staring at the sky. "You must touch him." She comes down to earth and grins. "That window is a disgrace," she says, then looks into the shadows. "This house is a mess all the way inside. It's forever since we cleaned up."

14.

Not long before my father died, he and I built a bonfire
of curved branches from a dead tree the wind had pulled
down. He was ninety years old, unsteady on his feet, in his last
winter. He climbed the hill face, undergrowth over rock, to
fetch the branches while I bucked the trunk, the heavy rounds
rumbling down into the clearing in front of their house,
Mother watching from the big window. We tended the blaze
all afternoon, Dad and I, speaking little, and in the dying light
my mother joined us. There we were, three winterers engaged
in small conversation, and I realized they had made me before
they knew how to make anything; that our triangle around
the fire was the cornerstone of what I had made, or told. The
flames flared with explosions as my father threw on heavy dry
limbs.

Almost sixty, I can still feel those rounds thudding, that
hefty cornerstone tipping. Even though I tried to make a fair
copy or facsimile or version or carbon of myself, of them, I've
sent only one true emissary into the world, a son, and he just
took off and vanished. The glass school was Emma's project.
Mostly I've just made stories, and this landmark I'm building
is probably not any kind of amazed unknowing, but hubris
pure and simple.

❧

Speaking of amazed unknowing, the night before he died
my father told me he was not my father, that my mother had

had a long-lasting affair that ran parallel to their marriage. Fantastical confession but credible because my father spoke it with such a sense of unburdening that there was an audible gasp that must have been air trapped behind the news. And then he fell asleep across the kitchen table and I had to carry him to bed, my mother fluttering moth-like around his intermittent breaths.

After the funeral my mother, in a moment of clarity, affirmed matter-of-factly that my father was Danny's father, whom I had known as a poetical unpractical rascally man long dead of an apparent aneurism, whose wife had quickly developed cancer and followed him. Small explosions in my skull for days, with unstable knickknacks falling from neural shelves and furniture items rearranging themselves. Fifty years ago my parents and Danny's had been close friends, but Danny and I were not almost cousins. We were brothers. Danny is childless, but he travelled a little, then came home to convert his barn and breed horses. Danny and I are brothers, but does he know? I will never ask him. Nor have I told Emma, for some reason.

∾

When we were kids, the route between my place and Danny's was a green tunnel in summer and the light at the end was yellow, his house at the top of its hill a faded wooden beacon.

I can't think about Danny without feeling anger and sadness.

When he left on his travels I was green, envious, lovesick, bereft, pathetic, because I could only stay home and listen to farmers' talk about the valley and the friable soil, the effect of salt on grapes. When he returned I could hardly look at him. When he returned to us, he was an unpredictable man who would disappear for weeks at a time, appearing at his parents' house half-starved, half-wild, to be only grudgingly taken in. He had no experience of tending vines. He knew of horses and about the sea. I only knew how to sit with aunts and uncles and tell them back the stories they'd told me. Summer nights when the highway was quiet, farmers met around a barbecue to plan the season and compare lives. I wandered among them collecting tales. Danny renovated his barn, tamed ponies, buried our father and then his mother. His wildness was locked away but you could sense it in him. When we were young men I wanted to see his secret valley, but when I asked he refused to take me with him across the plain to the mountains. And then Annie died and I began to dream up stories too complicated for any uncle or aunt to tell.

Danny has a wicked appetite.

Apocat feels sorry for me.

Winters, his barn was filled with ponies and horses and their foals; summers, Danny took the herd to the new corral by his broken cabin on a bench in the hills and left the homestead to mice and spiders. He preferred the company of ponies and horses to ours, though Tom and I drove out to see him once or twice. At his cabin we drank good wine, sang and told stories. When each of Tom's girls was born, Danny rode in to visit the family; he was welcome there. But he did not come to see Emma and me, even when Annie died, and we seldom spoke, except at Tom's from time to time.

Danny is a troubled man, Emma says, not right. A wife would have settled him into something like the rest of us, but it's too late now.

She broke her arm riding with him. She was drunk. This adventure continues to disturb me; I still feel a mixture of envy and admiration and excitement: a shaft of light piercing my own arm, just below the left shoulder, a bolt, nail, spear, arrow, sliver, and I fight sleeplessly with a ghost in our bed, listening to my wife's groans every time she tries to turn, as if a message from Danny is leeching through her, from far away, from the sea, from brandy, and I have been infected and must spend my night-time trying to read infection's signs around the village. And signs there are, not the least being Danny's illness and exile, James hanged, Abi's trouble, and no babies born since Tom's granddaughter last fall, and only Lucy and Abi with child, my biggest story rising, and great change lapping at the door and everything threatening to tumble with the rising ocean that when it ebbs will leave only islands and a sea.

∾

A rainbow spanned the dump. I was there spying on the three kids. What are they? What do they think? What's in them that's dangerous and tricky enough to ride out massive change? I sang Danny's adventures to my son. If a member of the audience warps the players by recording their acts, then praise or criticism of a player warps the witness. Once I held such things in memory, but now I have to write it down. I'm easily confounded by the children. Also I'm afraid in the attempt to settle everything I will miss the depths from which all arises. For me it is depth not height will tell the final truth, so my head is always down and I leave for others the sky.

~

My wife's pain from her broken arm and Danny's pain from his cancer, what do they signify? I wake in the dark to her moaning. I thought she was improving, but she is cocooned and ailing. It's so black. Where is the sun that has jurisdiction over human affairs? Where are the drugs to imbibe and get confused?

"Awake?"

"Yes," Emma says. Then, after a pause, "Can't you sleep?"

"The wall gives me no peace," I say.

"Poor sausage," she says, yawning. "And how much of our savings have you spent on those slabs?"

"Nothing. Not a cent."

"And the truck to bring them in?"

"Don't worry about money."

"Sure."

We get up before it's properly light and dress and go down to the kitchen and I fill Polly's water basin and she waddles over and drinks it dry in moments. It is her liver. Much water: much peeing. A green sign of her imminent end.

"I'm worried about the dog," I say.

We make coffee and spike it and take our mugs to the window and sit looking out.

"Apocat says we must touch our enemy."

Emma rolls her eyes. "Oh yes?"

"Her answer to the consortium."

"Ah," says Emma. "But what does it mean?"

"That's the question."

"What's the answer?"

I sit with Emma and we watch figures on the horizon hills: exactly like white horses, like white horses on the sea. I say I plan to import sand from the plain, lay a path beside the stone hedge, a sandy path to follow the wall's curve. Make a coastal walk through sand piled against a wall.

"We're supposed to live life, not storify it."

"Can't I do both?"

"Maybe not."

But it's useful dreaming. The wall begins at the corner of our house and runs in an imperceptible curve toward the western grape hills where my undisputed mother completes her days. It will end when I end. The sand walk is still an idea. I count the stones already laid and estimate how many years it represents. Stones help me live. Dust helps me sleep. My wall is for wind to find.

"What about Abi?" says Emma.

"Oh. I forgot to ask. How is she?"

"That girl has the weight of the world on her, but she is eating like a horse."

"That's good."

"She's practically living in Danny's barn."

"She's safe there."

"Danny's dying," Emma says.

"Yes, maybe he is."

"I've a feeling he won't come back."

"Sure he will."

"So. What do you think, Charles? Was it Danny or James?"

"Might be either."

∾

I know it was probably Danny. He and Abi rode north last summer, before James died. We watched them trot out together mornings, easy in their saddles, not talking, craggy cowboy and young girl, a sight to see getting smaller then vanishing beyond the cultivated hills, and vulnerable to speculation, our witnessing buoying them into the old seabed where, I suppose, they navigated the scattered stones and boulders, and their horses reunited with ghosts of their wild counterparts. And I saw it ring a change in Emma, the way they rode through the tall grasses, horses steaming, toward the mountains, because one day she too went riding with Danny — small, smaller, vanishing — got drunk, fell, broke her humerus, came home broken, changed, et cetera. What kind of apprenticeships are nurtured out there?

∾

Last night, I cooked dinner for my mother, then washed her feet as she crooned to herself something she'd learned as a girl: " . . . take down her combination and perform the operation, it's only human nature after all."

"What is the meaning of that?" I asked.

"Oh, you'll find out, tulip," she said. "When you're a man."

After clipping her claws, I patted dry her toes and asked if she wanted a drink.

"That wife of yours," she said, "is everything all right between you?"

"Of course."

"But she won't have another baby, will she?"

"Mom." I sipped my wine. "She's too old."

"No harm in asking."

"No point."

"Everybody's always fucking the wrong people," she said.

"What?"

"Danny's going to make millions," she said. "I hope you've thought it all out, Charles."

"Thought what out?"

"Never mind. Come and see the pigeons roosting."

I left my parents' house drunk on Dad's wine, and at home made love to my wife.

IV

15.

"It's fatal to leave the ethnographer out," he said.

"Fatal?" she said. "Come on. This village is devolving. Having no witness is hardly fatal. Anyway, it's done. We won't nail the funding."

"I've got the funding."

"Bullshit."

"True."

"We need a year."

"I've got us a year." He gave her a shrug. "And new parameters."

"Which are? What are you talking about?"

"I can't tell you yet."

"It's academic anyway. You screwed up."

"So to speak."

"You made a mess, my friend!"

"Okay, but let's be clear what's us and what's our work."

"That's not funny. You contaminated our research."

"Let's not run in circles. I have the funding. We have a new sponsor. You'll be the point person. They trust you. And, please, no talk about Maori facial tattoos."

∾

The ethnographers' second visit coincided with the start of spring and the first town hall meeting. While she met with the council and sat in on committees, he walked around the village alone, kicking his heels. They were guest speakers at a preliminary hearing at the hall, but she did the talking. They stayed a month in their tent on the common ground while worry in the town accelerated toward panic. Apocat and Kata invited him into their house to acquaint him with vernal customs and taboos.

∾

I sit at dawn by the wall wondering about all this. My dreams are violent (of Abi and Danny in his barn, she radiant, Danny radioactive) and all is rising, the sun over the village, teens by the river, shut-ins like my mother responding to news accounts of revolution and mayhem. I climb onto the wall and see, off in the distance, animals acting strangely, vicious oceans and rebels, reactors on fire, queer humans roaming the land, drifters and criminals released from jails and sanatoria hunting for refuge or their next cup of coffee. Abi will have her baby in a month, more or less, and what does it matter who is responsible? Already spring seems far removed from winter.

"What are you doing up there!" Emma calls out of the window.

"Looking for miners."

"You'll fall and break your back!"

Ashamed, I spread my arms as if to exclaim how fresh the air is on the raw top of my wall, then climb down and Emma brings out breakfast and we recline in the lee, eating cereal out of blue bowls. Black coffee in yellow mugs wait beside us on a warm flat stone while I ponder blue bowl, yellow mug, and where the stone will fit.

"It's important that we get in touch with everyone," Emma says. "No one must be left out."

"Some might prefer exclusion."

She makes an irritated sound. "Did you hear that howling?" she says.

"What howling?"

"It was howling. Very early."

"Coyotes?"

"I do not think it was coyotes."

"What then?"

"You do know James's folk have had to sell? You do know what's going on here, Charles? Some person was howling."

"Sometimes we cannot do otherwise."

She picks up the bowls with her good hand and hurries back inside.

～

Emma and I had a baby girl and boy but we lost her and he went away. That old hurtful news is loose again. Global catastrophe pales, our beautiful village pales. That what I did to protect my child was not sufficient, that George blames me for his sister's death; soon what we have lost and have yet to lose will be too much to bear. Coffee and a pipe filled with fresh tobacco, pungent, wafting, are a narrow path. The wall keeps chaos at bay but only for now. My disequilibrium must invent a new story, a fulcrum for the see-saw; name the children astride the ends Disaster and Exile. We must know the paternity of Abi's baby, otherwise it's secrets or immaculate conception and something truly spontaneous in the wings. I'm still suffering from my dad's confession; and why is it his? My mother should confess too, her statement of fact gives me no peace. I must get out and talk to the neighbours.

I still talk to Emma, of course, but our intercourse has more innuendo and less substance these days. We are growing old. I cannot ask her, *Do Danny and I look alike?* She diagnoses in me a minor depression. At noon I feel her watching from the house and feel pathetically reassured that my life has a witness, though I won't look back at her. We do not wear conviction on our sleeves, and I think we are not convinced of anything any more, except that we are afraid, then content, then afraid.

"Lunch time," she shouts. "In a minute," I say, and she replies, "If you don't come in now, you can make your own lunch."

"That's fine."

I roll a rock and right it tight in place. Fear's true enough — we flap our wings but do not try to fly — and the death of one's child is endless; our life is flawed by it; but insanity is beside the point.

Danny or James or, of course, the ethnologist.

I prowl the unfinished stone hedge, outside then inside. This wall is in service to no animal; this step after step circuit is vital to nothing; that a sand track will soon follow the wall, my footfalls growing softer and softer, advances no theory. Even so, nothing must interrupt my counting the stones in the possibility. *Possibility of what?* New evidence. *Evidence of what?* Not anxiety's geology. Not what's beneath the fear of learning death. These stones are ordinary stones but when you pass middle age eternity arrives, death without death. Dare I approach that shadow? Such thoughts. Death of a village, of a daughter is written somewhere, but I can't find the writing. Spring storms cannot blow away what I have done, and yet when my body steps bright from bed into a long parabolic view of the tree-lined street, neighbours leaning on their spades, I find it all so fragile I almost forget what Abi has to deal with, or my brother's last days, and on such mornings each stone loses its singularity as soon as it is placed. These are exceptional times. I've lost the thread of the story, replaced it with this rambling attempt to cover ground, replaced that with tears at such a transcendent image, and Emma curses from the open window those who wish to divide the villagers from the village, and beyond the wall clouds mass over the plain. I climb up again, weeping like a child, and see horse shadows, a goshawk — that's all I want to see — and pray for Danny's safe return.

∽

Pollen fills the air and a haze rolls down to the river where Apocat and Kata are walking for the first time this year to their tree. No sign of Double Mountain, but the blue sky presses down, impossibly clean, and tomorrow the volcano will be undeniable.

∽

"Are you ever coming in?" Emma asks.

"If George stayed in touch," I say, "things would be easier between us. If we knew where he was, say."

She sighs. "We agreed this was pointless."

"Yes. But."

"Your damned wall."

"This cursed wall."

She runs a finger along the tight crack between two stones. "We had our school."

"Yes, we did."

"Do you want to know what happened with Danny?"

"You told me."

"Not exactly."

"No?"

"I felt so young, Charles, when I was riding with Danny toward the mountains. Just for a moment. I felt brand new. And . . ."

"Yes?"

"A kind of ecstasy. Both of us."

"I thought you were going to say you . . . "

"I forgave myself."

"Did you forgive yourself, Emma?"

"That's why I fell."

∾

Emma leaves my side with a grunt and Polly follows her. I'm not sure what it is about truth. Clearly it promises to give us the perspective we want. I can recall Emma's face, such brightness, when we got married, her eyes when we met, the way her body stiffened when we lost Annie; these truths (if indeed they are separate) are as familiar as the view from this wall, yet there are new gaps in the landscape where names and paternities have come unstuck and been washed away by rain. How do I proceed? Lao Tzu left his home, stepped into the unknown; Jesus left disciples; Adi Sankara escaped the crocodile: they all vouchsafed the gatekeeper their discoveries. The wall advances stone by stone, dividing our house from the village. Birds visit, their chorus a deafening language I've never learnt. Our scientists are back, and other strangers, geophysicists as well . . . How can I not have known what

Emma had not told me? How can Emma not know what I have not told her?

∾

The air wet, green, distances submarine. Apocat and Kata say the black dog is a trick of the light and a portent. Angle of perception and the dog's tail confound the eyes, put its number of legs in question. Is that a dog? Is that a dog lacking a leg? A leg absent from birth? Has there been an accident? The apparition comes and goes and seems to thrive among the vines, shooting out on foraging missions, scuffling designs in the dirt. Polly does not even bark any more. A fleeting black *something* with three legs. A wildness attached to the village, and to Apocat and Kata, appearing in advance of the two women as if cognizant of their purpose and schedule, their route to the tree by the river and their path home, a wildness whose pattern is now discernable, that presages a new deviation.

16.

She let the horses out and spent the day with them, well, not with them, but getting her shoes wet and the legs of her jeans dirty while they ignored her. But they knew she was there, part of their world. All was easier outside now it was spring, except having a baby or dying, which wouldn't be easy anywhere any time. When it got dark, she leaned against Red's chest to hear his big lungs working. "I got a baby," she told him. "I won't go home, I'll never cross that little bridge again, I have quit my family."

∽

She lay in a nest of blankets on Danny's cot in a corner of the wind-creaking barn. Ghosts were flopping and bowing and having little fits up there behind the windows of his dead house. She could hear them ranting at each other in the dark.

She slept in her clothes: three baggy shirts, a pair of unbuttoned jeans.

∽

The barn empty of horses. Barn with early sun. Spider webs aglint in a draft. Fuggy smell of feed, hay. Not just a place: her home. By first light, after a long wakeful sleep, she felt like the youngest in a herd, a foal on the straw, brand new.

∽

She would not stay. She would run. She had to stay. She could not run. Danny would not come home and she would have to look after the horses forever. She had not been to school since the end of January. Her parents didn't care she was living with the horses. She was riding less. She was thin, except for her belly, feeding at Danny's desk on the soups and casseroles Emma left inside the barn doors. Soon she would run. But the horses.

One night for warmth and to challenge herself she slept in his ghost house, but the fire in the stove smoked and then went out, and she lay shivering on a split couch near the window, pigeons stepping over her. They found roosts on the plate shelf that ran around the room and she dozed off listening to them shuffling and scratching and ruffling their feathers. Something woke her in the dark and she got up and watched the barn, the sky, and a bright star eaten by clouds. A figure, head down, was trudging up the path with a heavy bag. A man slipping through the shadows toward the barn. She imagined James hanging alive, then dead. She did not want to see him, but mostly did not want his ghost to see her. When she looked again he had disappeared. A shiver ran up her spine.

The next day was cold; rainy wind was whistling under the sashes, wetting the sills. She stuffed a tablecloth in the broken window and went into the kitchen. The taps no longer worked. The kitchen was freezing and dim, the floor rough with dirt. Danny's money had dwindled. She counted the remaining bills, slipped them back into her pocket, the pigeons cooing, then walked the shabby hallway to the front door. Smell of mould. Patterns of green and black around a faint rectangle where a mirror used to hang. Probably no one had ever stood here and studied this little passage. She opened the door and wind sent her hair flying. There was someone on the path.

Not James. Harry. His bag looked heavy. She leaned on the wall and stared out. Hadn't there been a star in the middle of clouds? She shut the door and took quiet steps back into the house. A line of droppings marked the entrance to the front room. Finished with the place, she ducked her head and marched through the kitchen and let herself out the back door and locked it. She went round to the front, pushed the bills deeper into her jeans pocket. Harry was trotting up the path, his bag pitching him to the right.

"Brought you some things."

"Like what?"

"Sleeping bag. Air mattress. Camping stuff."

"What for?"

"I know you're camping out here." He stood in front of her like a dog, half-faithful, half-stupid. Staring at her, but being nice. Wind whistled in the loose porch railings. The steps were rotted through.

She hated Gee.

She didn't love Harry.

She'd dreamt she was flying on a beautiful white horse.

"Not here. The barn . . . "

He trudged back down the path, dropped the bag by the barn door, turned and left.

∽

Saint

The horses welcome her with their noses.
Danny lifted her onto her first horse.
Who bore her through shadows, eyes on the sea.

Each day she rides out, faster and farther.
Let me go blind, she says. Let me go deaf.
The barn safe at night, the horses like silk.

Under her fingers, their manes, their eyelids.
The baby draws blood and breath from her heart.
She feels their captivities align, align.

17.

When she was ten she read *Daughter of Dark*, and her sky-blue bike was a pinto called Light, which she amended to Leon in front of her friends, and she rode Light from the glass school up a row of vines, down another, once round the village, always winding up at the barn from where came thuds and low voices in early morning and evening; but if she arrived during the day she found a thick dusty aromatic silence.

She has just repeated the identical journey on a real horse and Red feels supple and both of them are smooth with sweat, up against the sunny side of the barn, away from the wind and from the sad eyes of Danny's house. The sea after a storm. She breathes in his smell. Down there the river loops like writing or a wide silver snake, and the other horses run their own circles and loops in the riverbank pasture.

She lets go the reins and wraps her arms around his neck.

Red drops his head and drinks from the trough.

∾

All winter of her tenth year she wobbled and skidded on ice and gravel on her new mountain bike, blinking ice crystals from her eyes, imagining slipping under the wheels of a semi-trailer plunging down the highway, yes, no, yes, no, horrendous squeals and blasting horns, *roll like a hamster, roll away from the traffic, roll into the ditch,* and no one saw her, only truckers and long-distance travellers. She rode the soft shoulder until she was shaking, then returned home. Safe yet.

∾

"Stand at his withers and take his mane, gently."

∾

She dreamed about James and Gee leaping off a cliff; down below were waves and rocks; they spread their arms to slow their fall.

She worried about her thinness, more a slenderness and a knot. Once she met Harry on the barn path and hid her belly, tired of explaining. They went to the schoolyard to talk and Gee was there. She and Gee smoked hash on the tip of a cigarette. Harry took a cigarette but refused the hash. Gee laughed at her baggy coat, laughed and couldn't stop. She went home stoned and snuck in and drank a bottle of wine and some vodka and went blind and her father put her to bed. When she woke up, her face was blue in the mirror.

∾

"Stand in the stirrups and give him his head."

∾

Not flying but thundering toward something, into something, and not alone, not thinking, riding hard into those mountains: she is significant. Racing away from what she knows, dividing what she knows into girl/horse, baby/man, girl/baby.

Horse shadows and joy. She is a horse girl. She is bliss. She rides Light, no, Leon. She mourns Tortoise. She rides big Paraclete. She rides her own Red. She loves to ride Red, afraid of being thrown, wanting to be thrown. She rides the hermit horse, Solomon, more safe, less often. She rides Red who sees through her. They are inseparable under a sky pouring water she knows and water she's never felt, never any closer to the mountains. She rides the horses one after another, her weight-distribution and shape weird. Horses she has never met, has no memory of learning. Horses that will never fill with rain. She rides an hour and pauses at a hollow rock that holds dark snowmelt, so Light, no, Leon, no, Red, can drink.

∾

She rides Red into the mountains to find the pass — there will be something, some weather or light peculiar to the place that she can wrap around the child she's carrying.

∾

Everywhere were signs of spring, ice cubes in the river, tracery on the poplars. She reined Red in, returned him to the barn, stoked the stove, brushed the horses, talking to them.

18

"What did you say?" asked Abi.

"What?" Harry posed like a discus thrower, then skimmed his rock off the poisonous water against the engine block of a half-sunk truck.

"What did you say?"

"I didn't say anything."

"You said something."

"Did I?" He spun another stone; it bit a splash from the surface, rattled off the engine and fell back with a plop. "That's my life — clink clank plop."

"At the end you sink."

"Are you going to tell me who it was?"

"No."

"Have you told anyone?"

"What does it matter?"

Harry spun another stone and it sank without bouncing. "I'm going to the other side." He pointed to this and that bit of junk, stepping places to the far cliff. "Hippity-hop. Watch this."

She paid attention to his long thin big-boned body as he made the cliff in several leaps — refrigerator to boulder to chassis to engine block to wheel-rim to a curving platform of roof shingles beneath the overhang. Once there, he crouched and called: "Lots of room. Come on over. It's a little island."

The dented fridge was yellow-green. She'd change places with her baby if she could, if that was possible. Couldn't they switch? She closed her eyes. To float in an inner world. Wobbly boulder, narrow chassis, wheel-rim. But they were like horse and rider, fastened into their places, into who they were. If she was winter, the baby was summer out of spring. She was feeling so pregnant — not simply pregnant, but complicatedly pregnant. Somehow all boys and men were hurt by this baby. Her baby was no lie, but she had to nurture lies and keep guessing where it came from when she didn't even know. She might talk to the man she'd called Uncle all her life, but he was in hospital and she couldn't visit him because she was so big and it was too far for her to travel.

It was easy to get to where Harry was, although she wobbled on the boulder. In the shadow of the cliff were drawings, it looked like, etched or sprayed onto the rock. She really wanted to talk, but didn't know what to tell and doubted Harry's ability to listen. He was lost in his purpose, hunched over with his back to her, busy with the cliff-face, and she was lost in hers.

She couldn't see what he was doing, but the place was peaceful. The asphalt tiles they stood on were layers deep, all different colours. *Tell him.* She wanted to. She felt betrayed by his ignoring her. Wanted to talk to him.

"What will you do when you finish school?"

Harry was adding his own marks to the others on the rock. "We're only in Grade 10, Abi," he said. He whipped off his toque, and flicked it to her and she sat down on it. She was shaking; her shoulders were shaking. She let the shake turn into a shudder. She felt weak, watery, bloated, sitting on the tiles. With the sun low in the sky the pond was in shade. Only the tops of spiky new grass and metal parts sticking up out of the water were lit. She laid her hand on the cold surface of a bent filing cabinet and squinted through her hair at the boy at the cliff face. The scene transformed: instead of a dump with the scattered castoff goods of the village, the place was gloriously red and ancient. Edges vibrated and there was symmetry to everything.

"Are you okay?" Harry asked.

"No."

She went to stand beside him and they drew simple animal outlines on the cliff face with bits of iron. Fish. Bird. Cow. Snake. Tufts overhead caught the sun; the tufts were like small ruby-green creatures rearing against the blue evening sky; long brambles looped down.

A bird landed to her right and she closed her eyes to listen to it hopping, scuffling in the crusty tiles. "Crow," she whispered.

"Huh?" said Harry.

"I know we're only in Grade 10," she said, "but I still ask the question. What will you do?"

"I don't know what I'm going to do. What are you going to do?"

She didn't answer, but felt tiny surges and questings of the small limbs inside her womb.

"What are you going to do?" he repeated. "You know."

A train whistle blew, train rushing down the line from the west, and they both looked up.

"What did you and James talk about that night?" she said.

"Something," he said. "He was loaded."

"Something about me?"

"No. Someone else. James was really wrecked," Harry said. "Bent out of shape."

"Who did you talk about?"

"Stuff."

"Was it me?"

"Yeah."

"What was it about?"

"Nothing. I don't know. I promised not to say anything."

She opened her eyes to a robin using its beak to forage through last year's leaves. "It doesn't matter now, does it?"

"I didn't believe him anyway," he said.

"How about yourself?" she said. "Do you believe in yourself? Do you?"

Harry was looking at her, puzzled, his face in a beam of sun, mouth curved in a pained expression. "Yes. Sure I do."

She scratched a mouth on the cliff face. "I bite my tongue all the time — you know that expression? I used to hate everything, but now . . . "

"I'll tell you one thing," he said. "You are the only person I have ever felt comfortable with."

The robin found a bug. She heard the crunch. The bird cocked its head at her and said: *You are no great maker of future plans*, then flew low along the shore of the pond, lifted and vanished over the cliff.

She watched buds explode into white blossoms over Nuisance Island. They wanted light. They wanted sun. Every morning she felt less and less safe: James here or James gone, Danny here or Danny gone, the ethnologist here or gone, Harry here or gone — amounted to the same thing: into her belly had poured a sharp fluid and now life was unstoppable.

༒

"Now rowel the horse on!"

❧

All around was the yellow-green world. She was on her way. She carried a baby she wanted. She was getting used to herself, forgetting to ask, *Why am I so young? Who is the father? Who will help me? What should I do?* She wrapped her fist round the horse's mane and leaned in to smell him. She and Red were facing the mountains now, swirled round by steam. The smell was leather and sweat. The kid was sleeping in her belly, his fists closed. Back in the village people wandered back and forth.

19

What is the relationship between our village and these thrown-away things? Did the village become lighter, less substantial, more joyful as the dump grew in size? And do we unbalance our world when we deem the rag-pickers rags? Now abandoned, the dump is more symbol than fact. We should look into what the village has lost, what we have collectively given up. Yes we should.

I don't believe that only strangers can see what's broken down. We are inbred, it's true, but surely we are adaptable and capable. When we filled the swamp with refuse, we found another location.

∾

At the beginning of time, after the first summer, we were all flying through the wilderness, founding villages. We had been holidaying in the mountains, valley to valley, following our noses, and then wind filled the trees and it got cold, so we took a path beside a stream and found a river that led to a dry meadow in a coulee of scrub teeming with antelope and set to work.

∾

We are survivors, castaways, searching the horizon for our ship, a steamer, liner, cargo vessel, fishing boat, tug, trawler, launch, dinghy, barge, ferry, tanker, raft, freighter, rowboat, but the sea is empty. We are sailors, bridge officers, engineers, stokers, deckhands hard at work, chartless stowaways, far from land. We are landlocked riders with a hard gallop ahead but alive, transfigured, in relationship.

∾

We live between our village and the land. What we have cultivated in the long view of mountains will vanish in the next human empire — a vast surface mine maintained by monster machines. Our next enterprise will have nothing to do with horses or the soil, only with machines and rock; our tribe will winter by tropical seas to escape such violent tedious labour.

20.

My heart leapt when I saw Danny walking slowly down the road and I ran out to greet him. He said the trip to the sun and back had been easy, but the waiting with other sufferers in a corridor among potted trees and cheerful nurses, views of endless roofs, water courses, golf hills, speeding highways, long evenings in the hotel room and forced marches through the city had weakened his spirits.

He was pale and irritable and still had cancer.

"I've been amazed by horses all my life," he said. "I mistook them for humans. I was not wrong. How is Emma?"

"Her arm's better, but she still can't lift anything."

"She fell off Paraclete, Charles. That's a long fall. I'm going home to lie down."

21.

He kept dreaming of that early spring camping trip through the basin-land, thirty-five years ago, his first pony in that meadow between two hills. Longing, granddam of Paraclete. His hand on her flank. Rainbow over the pass. The first stars.

In today's brief canter he'd twisted in the saddle and pulled a muscle near his heart, may have been his heart, and had smoked two joints. His thighs ached as he crossed through the vines back to the homestead. He would never forget the rope, crusty polypropylene, its fibres cutting into the boy's throat. James' body depending from this rope tied to a thick branch. New limbs, new muscles. What other chores had occupied the yellow rope? What had scarred and busted its petro-chemical strands? What vehicles had it towed, luggage tied down, what jetsam had it held together? The rope had had no smoothness left in it, despite the strain. He felt faint after the long weeks in the city, but the radiation in itself had been nothing and scopes showed the tumour reduced and in all just being home made him generally feel whole again, though still not able to figure out what had happened, except resentment had been burned out of him; errant cells were on the run; the surgery date was set. What should he do next? It wasn't impossible to call it off, the operation, call it a day. He still had strength to ride north on a fierce little horse. The last wild pony he'd brought in had fought him all the way. Her grown foals were down there in the barn. Abi had taken good care of them. He hadn't seen the girl yet, but there was evidence of her squatting with them in the barn. He thought about her all the time. Her face. Her knees. Her eyes watching him through a curtain of hair. All the clichés. It was the image of this girl that kept him going, the way she looked, sounded, sat a horse. She'd materialize at odd moments. On his way to and from the hospital. In the eyes of young nurses. In their bodies. A child with lovely simple perfect lines. Yearling. Expectant. Unaccountable. He still desired life, apparently.

Lying in the room with the radiologist at his side, he'd decided to be positive, to fight the good fight, turn resentment into anger, a white-hot variety, let lust focus the fury and split lust's aim from Abi's image, set it at the illness. In his head, was it all? Was the journey almost over? To hell with Charles and his stories. He would not go where he was going, not toward death, but along a path between lust and fear, a windy ride through the plain, race to the tree-lined finish, pin the tail on the gatekeeper and pop through the trapdoor to land on baskets stuffed with what? Here's a policeman, here's a police bike. Here's a cowboy and here's a horse. Here's a head and here's some long black shiny hair. Sleek and bouncy, the young nurse on duty weekends. Match horses to their eyes, eyes to bodies, sailors to the sea. Recurring dreams in which Abi seemed a golden figure on the horizon or a ribbon that fluttered in his wake like an afterburn.

∾

The horses were fine. Abi was in the barn, sitting right where he'd left her weeks ago, now very pregnant. He was almost sad to see her there, though he'd planned the moment and what they'd say.

"What've you been up to?"

"I go to the dump sometimes with Harry."

"Yes? After school?"

She sat on a bale. "After my chores with the horses. I go riding every morning."

"Who?"

"Red. All the others."

"Should you do that?"

"I don't care."

"Your parents?"

She shrugged, kicking her heels against the straw.

"Well, there you are," he said. "You're more and more like me."

"Can we go back to the cabin?"

"Should you ride that far?"

"For sure."

"Why do you want to?"

"It's peaceful there. Can you ride?"

"Sure. I've been out already. I pulled a muscle." He laughed.

"What was it like, the hospital?"

"A lot of waiting around."

"They took it all out?"

"Not yet. They shrank it, I guess, so the surgery date's set." He got up and crossed the barn's dusty floor. "You've been living here."

"Yeah. Are you scared?"

"Oh, yes."

"But you don't want to be dead."

He smiled.

"I think the horses missed you," she said.

"I'm glad to see them."

"I'll still help."

"I know. That's good. But you've got your own problems."

"Can we ride to the pass?"

"The cabin won't be easy. The pass is too far."

"Okay. When can we go to the cabin?"

"Don't know. What's the big hurry?"

She wrinkled her nose at him and joined him at the door, staring out. A storm was gathering in eerie silence: forked lightning illuminated low black clouds boiling above them — not a blade of grass or a branch moved.

"It's just like the only thing," she said. "The only thing I feel like doing."

V

22.

This is the little stone with which I have conversations, this round, volcanic, well-smoothed black stone that Danny brought me from the sea, that fits into my palm. What's given away flourishes. What's not told rots. This stone is the mother of the present wall. This stone contains the village's fortune, if only I could read it. Before tragedy, before I began to know where I could and could not go, I held onto this stone. A moment ago the stone was cold, even with the summer's heat, but it has warmed in my hand, and now I curl my fingers around a single thought with red veins. We lost our daughter. We started a school. We lost a son who might return. I have a brother who is dying.

❧

When my path crosses Abi's, I see a contained girl containing and wonder how this place, once a frontier, now an anachronistic pocket, appears to her. How does our village affect her? She's not the first mother this young, nor the last, but our insular spirit, unfed by recent travel, untrusting (because without perspective), cannot bear to register that she's pregnant. I am not a seer or mystic — leave that to the weavers by the river — yet it seems we must keep Abi safe until our several-fold issues (nerves, fear, boredom) are passing weather. We used to produce in our children something unique and durable, and the village was built on that capital. Abi carries our last interest, our latest child.

∾

Tom has just brought me several bags of dusty sand and I have raked it into the lee of the home portion of wall and marched back and forth like a soldier on guard, tamping it down. The work is going well and the sand laps against the large bottom stones. Will I advance the wall next or the path? Will the path follow the wall or the wall the path? For now the partially built wall determines the path of the path, but there is no reason not to continue the path and then erect the wall along its length. But am I a creature who sets a plan and follows it? Sand is more flexible than stone. Without the wall, the sand will blow away. Sand is the time-infected progeny of stone. Stone is space-challenged sand. Sand whistles, sinks, shifts, drifts, stings, slips, softens. Stone calls us back. Sand gets in your eyes, ears, genitals. We approve of stone and want sand controlled, held, dyked.

"Don't forget to count the grains," Emma calls from the house. "It's in the Bible. Go on."

Or am I the kind of hero who looks for a plan in what is already aligned? Shouldn't a hero just get on with things? I've lived here all my life and known nothing of other places; I rarely speak at meetings; but I have sent tidings of our village to the outer world and have built a wall to divide nothing from nothing that will always be unfinished.

We are running out of sand and drowning in bits of information.

I send my wife a vigorous wave. I thank the gods every day for Emma, without whom I would go on like this, thought by thought, with no compass, forever. Who thinks me foolish. Who sends me out to the garden, signals me from the house, brings me a sandwich. At night she wraps herself around me, her belly soft against my behind.

"Sometimes you look so sad out there," she whispers. "How is it going?"

"As you see." I put my nose under the covers. "We churn in our own darkness."

She growls. She nips my neck. We understand each other.

"I was jealous, I suppose," I say. "Danny has a tattoo low on his belly. He showed me."

Emma bites my shoulder. "But *my* rival is a wall."

23.

The hall stage was crowded with strangers, men and women in suits, while the villagers, local farmers, businessfolk and union people sat on white plastic chairs that at night formed towers to the rafters on either side of the gallery. The union members arrived in buses from the south wearing green T-shirts and sat stiffly beside the protestors of our village and neighbouring communities and outlying farms. Many of our crowd sported neon-orange shirts, something Emma had sorted out. Apocat and Kata's cousins from the reserve sat in the back row, along with Pete Milkmemory. An early fog dimmed the room, of panic, anticipation, anger, greed and matter-of-fact conciliation. Cigarette smoke hung about the entrance.

Tom stepped to the microphone at the edge of the stage and said, "This meeting is to discuss the proposed quarry mine."

Scores of union members cheered.

A thickset man with a beard and a belly got to his feet. "There will be a hundred and fifty high-paying jobs on this rock mine." He paused and squinted. "Such as would bring such relief to this recess-battered region!"

Opponents of the quarry raised their arms and booed.

A man in a white shirt and a yellow tie got up. He approached the microphone. He said in a low voice that a health study sponsored by the province showed that the quarry would lead to a hundred and seventy additional deaths in the region, many respiratory-related. "Supporting this project is tantamount to being a friend of cancer," he murmured. And then his voice quavered. "Blasting and dust from the mine would poison our air and devastate the region's wineries. It would *increase* unemployment. It's not a partisan issue. It's not about politics. It's about protecting the good lives and jobs we already have . . . preserving quality of life. It's that simple."

"The village is dying, man!" shouted a voice.

Tom introduced the spokesman for Wildland Construction, the China-based firm proposing the quarry. The man waited and, when the crowd had quietened, he said, "That study is suspicious and ludicrous. Part of our plan is to divert the highway away from the town. The Air Quality Management folk we have talked to say that our plan for the rock mine will not significantly increase highway truck traffic, and overall will improve regional air quality. All our studies have concluded that the mine will not endanger the health of residents in surrounding communities. This is not the first quarry we've launched. This is the right project, in the right place, at the right time. The quarry will bring in an estimated two billion in sales tax over the life of the mine as well as create hundreds of indirect jobs. Our five-thousand-acre quarry will yield about eight hundred million tons of granite over the next hundred years."

"Yeah," said Tom, taking the microphone, "and leave behind a hole fifteen hundred feet deep and four miles long. All the aggregate mined from the site will be trucked to the coast, to cities. Why should we sacrifice our beautiful and pristine plain to feed the aggregate demand of next century's mega cities?"

One of the union members stood. "I'm forty," he said, "and I've been out of work for three years. We're talking about jobs, about putting guys back to work. This is a job I could get."

Danny, from the back of the hall, called out: "I live within sight of the place Wildlife wants to mine. They're misrepresenting the facts. People in this town want their land left the way it is."

"You've sold your place already, Danny-boy!"

The Wildlife rep jumped up. "This land is crown land. It does not belong to the village."

The government woman stood and bowed. "Yes, that is right."

"They're a billion-dollar transnational corporation that just wants its way."

"That plain is where life was created," called Kata. "It is a sacred place. Chief, please talk to them."

"We have a moral decision to make," Tom told the crowd. "It should be based on respect for religion and history. We should reject this massive quarry."

"No," said the Wildlife spokesman.

His supporters roared.

He held up a hand for silence. "What we are talking about is an essential source of ingredients that will feed the region's economic ascent. Most of the vineyards will be fine."

"How can it reduce highway traffic? How can you say to us there won't be health hazards and environmental destruction?"

"Our town is known for its grapes, for the beauty of its vineyards."

"Where will workmen and their families live?"

"Save us from conservative politics!"

"Take it to the Board of Supervisors!"

"Put it to the vote!"

Chairs screeched on the floorboards. The orange shirts and green T-shirts were roiling in opposition.

The Indians from the reserve sat in silence.

"This vote will be a watershed moment for us," shouted Tom. "We've seen land all around us go to mining, microwave towers, landfills, prisons and other horrible so-called necessities."

"I didn't think the village was organized enough to really fight any change," Lucy said to Emma.

"We can't stick at what we wanted to be fifty years ago," Emma said. "We have to change. But not this. Not this."

A new figure stood from the table on the stage, a lanky young man with hair tied back in a ponytail and wearing a suit that looked too small for him. He stood at the microphone. "If I might have your attention."

"Who the hell are you!" yelled Danny.

"That's the tent man," Emma said.

"I am one of the scientists who camped here last year," the young man said. "I'm speaking as a consultant to Wildlife. Please — " He held up his hands to quiet the boos. "There has been an influx of upscale housing and care-homes in your neighbouring counties — in towns and villages closer to the cities — over the last fifty years. The first people who moved out here were politically and economically conservative and vocal and the NIMBY attitude was very strong. It overwhelmed the natural openness and vitality of village life. Where there was successful opposition to major mines, to jails and similar employers, villages became bedrooms to the city and retirement centres. My partner and I have studied these communities. Broadly speaking, most now look like soulless ghost communities. You will be next, but you do not need to go down that road. Towns that have seen the light and welcomed mines and such sources of blue-collar jobs into the region have experienced a new spirit of revival. There is a healthy bustle in these towns. When much of the workforce has only a high school diploma, there's the sense of family and the sense of possibility. There's a real community, instead of a retirement or bedroom community."

The Wildlife spokesman leaned over the microphone and smiled. "Wildlife Construction," he said, "built a five-hundred-acre rock mine on Loaf Mountain over in the southwest corner of the province."

"That is so," continued the young man. "The town there was formally an upscale suburban haven, and that mine has now attracted thousands of new families into those quiet neighbourhoods. Property values have risen. That mine has filled those good schools and gentle hills with a fresh generation of kids."

"Indeed," said the spokesman. "Let me recap. It is quite simple. We will extract almost a billion tons of granite over the next century, supplying building material to other booming towns and cities. The final result, by the end of the century, will be a deep lake — plenty of water for the irrigation of crops and the potential for hydro power. In the meantime, plenty of jobs."

"That's bullshit! What about light-radar robot trucks? There won't be any jobs in a couple of years!"

A thin man in a green T-shirt climbed onto the stage and stood shaking in front of the microphone. "I am an unemployed labourer. I am thirty years old. I have two kids. I grew up a mile from the proposed mine site, and now live in the city. I am two weeks away from losing my house and car. We need these projects to happen now. I just want to come home."

"I speak for the wineries, and I vote yes," came a voice from the table.

Representatives from local school districts, tourism councils, and chapters of the Sierra Club spoke in favour of the mine.

"I have a list, everyone," called Dmitri. "Grape growers, teachers, the principal are all for the mine and so am I. Billion dollar transnational, so what? Wildlife will win!"

Locals whistled.

"What about our sacred land?" said Kata. "Chief Pete?"

Chief Pete Milkmemory stood up. He was as old as the sisters and wore beaded slippers and a red, white and black headdress. In one hand he held a tapered wooden peg, and in the other a small pelt.

"Yes," he said. "We only have one creation site. Only one. It's like your Garden of Eden." He looked out of the hall window to the north. "Once it is destroyed by a mine, it's gone. The site of the proposed mine is the place where all life was created."

"But you've applied for a permit to build a four-star resort casino!" called the Wildlife rep.

The Chief turned slowly around. "I can't remember the first time I rode a horse," he said. His wide eyes stared ahead and his voice grew firmer as he continued. "We made a circle when the grass is brown. I will not talk here about the circle, but there were thousands of horses. We know the old ways will be forgotten. The wild horses are dangerous to people . . . We will not leave. If we go away we will always come back." He shuffled into the aisle and held up the peg and the skin. Above his eyes, white discs with red centres revolved, dangling black beads trembled.

The band rose en masse and chairs clattered and the men and women began a rhythmical hymn, and the boards shook with their stamping.

Tom tapped the mike. "There are just too many uncertainties for me," he said. "This vote is about the right to determine what happens in our community."

I helped Tom and Harry stack the plastic chairs. Locals gathered out in the parking lot dust as buses carried the union members away.

∾

I dreamed my wall was falling, the house full of water, and I was watching Danny from the glass room lose his footing and tumble into the dark thick loamy flood and Abi, all pale limbs, was swimming to rescue him, trying to haul him toward the house, and I jumped out of the window, down into the water, and he floated up in my arms, his face bony, his left eye shrunken shut, his right looking into my eyes, and there was no sign of the girl.

The future is an abstraction — like waiting in the dark to tell a story when there's no one there, or writing in the dark, the words only legible when the light comes, a candle or the sun-up — and the past never began.

I tried to speak, to articulate something profound, at our last emergency meeting. It had been discovered that Wildlife might be planning to relocate the town, lock, stock and barrel, and Emma had sent out a shrill email, but only a few people showed up. Present were Apocat and Kata, Harry and Gee, Tom and Lucy with their new baby girl, all their daughters, even Abi. Had there been a family reconciliation? The ethnologists sailed in late with a handful of others. I knew there were ghosts among us and that they would have the most to say if we were quiet enough to make out the words. I said something like, "If we could just get perspective we could put it all together. But we never quite manage perspective, do we? We are always acting out of what we do not know." Emma was looking at me with compassion and pity. I saw the way Abi gazed at the young ethnologist. I had expected blame and hatred, but found only sorrow. Even Kata and Apocat were cowed. We call for forgiveness and hang up. We send unsigned confessions. We drive past in trucks, tanks, sportscars, speedboats, bicycles, semi-trailers, and shout apologies that are lost in the wind. We run as long as we can. We die arms open, only children leaping a rift from one country to another. We cut ourselves off from the mothering past in order to advance, but lose touch with the ground. The dark warm land behind us sticks to our spines as our heads swivel mid-leap. Eventually it will be death because the sky's claim is too powerful. But for now we must fly or fall.

24.

"Not James, then?"

"Not him."

"Not Harry."

"No."

Abi and her father stood poised in the centre of the living room. Their arms at their sides. Spring sunshine lit motes around them.

"A man, then, not a boy?"

"Maybe."

"Take your time."

"Don't coach me."

"There's no rush, that's all."

"That's not the problem."

"What's the problem?"

"You will make up your mind."

"I'm your dad."

"So?"

"I just need to know from you."

"And then what?"

"That depends."

"It just happened."

"Tell it."

"I can't."

"Oh, sweetheart."

∾

"It's done, okay? It doesn't matter."

"Once we know, your father and I, you will be safe and we will raise this baby together."

"No."

"What else then?"

"I want a different choice."

"Once everything is settled, you can work for different choices. Children are like a promise to that. But right now you must tell us and let us look after you and the baby."

They sat facing each other, Abi on her bed, Lucy on a chair by the door, heaped clothes between them.

"Why must I tell you?"

"What happened to you was wrong."

"I just want you to leave me alone — both of you. Leave me alone."

∾

"I don't want surgery."

"Will you die if you don't have surgery?"

"Probably. Maybe."

"You don't know."

"If I die, I die."

They sat their horses by the barn door and watched the plain shifting under the turbulent sky.

"Sometimes you don't seem any older than me."

"Right. Don't slump, Abigail. Keep your back straight."

∾

"The mountains look pretty far."

"Can you ride that far?"

"I can if you can."

"When we get going, we'll feel better, I'm sure."

"I don't want anyone but you when the time comes."

"Why?"

"Because you don't judge."

"I'll tell you something. I have never felt this ill."

"Such a frail human being."

"Such a sturdy girl. When I look at you I am so aware of beauty."

"Let's go."

"Sure."

"I mean let's really go."

∽

"I'm trying to remember a place. When I was young. A beach on a small island, hot and calm. Waves like little feet on the sand. The sun on rotting weed . . . "

"Mmm."

"I can smell it now. Sulphur, salt."

"Uh-huh."

They'd left the village before dawn and were through the vines before the first birds began to sing. The blue sky mixed up with black and white clouds. The morning chill lifted as they moved north, Danny on Solomon, Abi on Red, two packhorses and the rest in a string behind them. Slow, rhythmic hooves on the packed ground.

∽

They slept at his cabin, squalls passing overhead. They watched sheets of rain to the north and south and the room crackled with electricity.

Abi wanted to tell him he was one of three, but was afraid to say the words. She said she didn't want him to die.

"I know," he said.

"And I love this."

"Yeah," he said. "There's room to breathe."

"Why does no one live here?"

"The Indians do." He waved his arm toward the reserve, the smoke from a few fires hanging above the community.

"Because we put them there," she said.

"Yeah. This is a poor land. Farming didn't work out. Those who tried vanished in famine and locusts."

"Before I was born."

"Before I was born," he said. "Are you getting what you want, Abigail?"

"Yeah. This is pretty good."

∾

They stayed at the cabin all next day while rain poured from the sky. Toward sunset the clouds peeled away from the west horizon and sun shot through the plain.

"Do you want to go home?"

"Maybe."

"Last chance."

"I'm scared."

"We'll go back in the morning then."

"No."

"What, then?"

"Keep going."

"You ready for the tent?"

"I'm not ready for anything," Abi said. "But I've got you to help me."

"Good."

Up at dawn, Danny had the horses organized by the time Abi was awake. They cooked and ate oatmeal without speaking. They mounted and left. They rode through rain and sunshine and had the tent up by noon, both quiet and exhausted.

∽

A long night of rustlings and coyotes circling, calling, rain on the tent roof. Fear of miscarriage. Fear of death. Intercostal muscle or heart attack; indigestion or miscarriage.

∽

Abi watched him climb into the saddle. It looked painful.

He turned. "I see you're up, Ms Slip-Slop."

"I feel like I'm in a dream."

"You're still going to have a baby."

"Anyway." She got to her knees looked up into his eyes. "How far to the pass?"

"Depends." He glanced round, then said, "Should we expect your dad with a shotgun?"

"It's not yours."

"I dreamed he was after us."

"This is nothing like what I thought it would be. I'm looking at you and thinking that you're just a boy."

"I'm not a boy."

"No. Anyway, it's not yours."

∽

"I can talk to you. No one has ever listened to me the way you do."

"Not mine, then — "

"No."

"No?"

"No."

"Then I don't understand why you should be in my life now I am old and sick and–"

"Why do you need to understand?"

"I don't need to, but don't you want me to?"

"We are doing it. Running away. We're going."

"Yeah. It's a foolhardy idea."

"It's what you want, right? What both of us want. You always said that."

"Sure."

"The horses love it."

"Except they won't survive without us."

"How d'you know?"

"They're no longer wild."

"But you did that. You brought the ponies back. They can go wild again. If they can survive, we can."

"Ah, Abi. I don't know if we can survive."

"How d'you know what will happen? You don't know."

"I can't get away from my illness and you can't escape your baby."

"So we don't make it. We're doing something. Nothing's perfect anyway."

He smiled. "I will die out there and your baby will come."

"You'll deliver my baby and I will die and you'll have a baby to look after."

"You will have twins and we'll both die."

"Oh my God. Twins?"

"Yes."

"The ponies are going home."

"True."

"And we brought a lot of food."

"True."

"Is there really a valley full of animals?"

"Yeah."

"We can drink from ponds and streams."

"Yep."

"We'll find out about ourselves."

"Everything perfect."

25

The sun came up over Double Mountain, the volcano, the peaks pink, the other mountains to the west starting to glow. Danny and Abi rolling up their sleeping bags, packing their tents, loading the horses, were asking for something new, their tasks prayers, and there in the morning was a scarf of pure light and all else grey and pewter. Dark going away. Light forming above the plain. Over the invisible cities, the sea and islands. A smell of green in the unsullied alpine air and the sun a molten ball.

Then they were in the foothills and saw signs of wild ponies, folded grass in moist hollows where they had lain the night before. Many birds sang and flocks were rowing overhead, tier after tier, going the way they were going.

They rested at noon, continued in a leisurely way into evening. They walked in sleepy silence, then camped while there was still light enough to explore where they were.

∽

Mornings were for speaking. Mornings were slow walking conversation. The packhorse Concordance clanged with pots and pans. Abi's thighs ached.

"Will we get to the pass today?"

"No, not today, Abi."

"You know what to do, right?"

"I know what to do, sure. I've delivered foals. I know how to do this."

"Okay."

"Do you regret what we're doing?"

"No."

"There is something I must tell you."

"Sounds like I may not want to hear."

"I sold my land. The money is all for you. The money's back there waiting."

"We are not going back."

"That's fine, but that's only one story. Another sees you living with twins near the sea."

"Not likely."

"There." He pointed north at the dark slash. "That's our lives just ahead."

∽

Once he could taste the mountains, Danny stopped worrying about the journey and what they had agreed to do. The idea to let anything happen, as long as they had food and shelter, seemed accountable, a number. They were together and alive and he felt his health returning, and they often walked side by side, resting the horses, as they travelled toward the pass and the valley beyond.

∽

Abi felt herself getting lighter, her limbs flying away, as the baby grew heavier, but somehow her feet kept hitting the ground and sending her forward and the man at her side was a friend and the horses were like a continuous wall, steady and faithful. If only it could be like this, a long walk that ended in sleep that led to another walk toward those mountains. This wasn't what James had chosen or what the village had chosen.

Why should she want a complicated future? A voice kept asking: *So, sexy, what have you done now?* and then silence, hers and his. This morning she'd felt invisible. Sunlight had shone through the blue tent walls. Crows shrieking. His eyes hooked into hers, looked away, and all was joy.

Her baby would die and she would die, one after the other. Why must the order be discovered? She was not ready. She was ready. How can three into one equal one? Easy. The day slowly drained of light. She sank into the earth, sifting through castle, childhood, dragon, to lie on the floor of her bedroom while her dad and mom and her sisters came and went, still with no idea of what was about to happen.

∾

It started to rain. A steady drilling downpour. Everything that frightened her was hissing beside them noisy as a rebel army. Soon the earth was a skin of thick purling water built of knife-sharp, uncombinable standing oblongs. No one back in the village had a clue. They were all talk. They knew nothing. And Abi and Danny rushed on in silence, the glassy oblongs writhing up against their dirty boots as they went on, the horses quietly following. *Oh, the rebels have us by the throats.* At every rise there was a pause. Abi gasped, and the oblongs squeaked.

∾

Such beauty in the early sky after a night in the open, smoke plumes on the south horizon, rising to the cloud gap and that belt of warm blue light.

26.

The end is not the beginning even though that's what it seems. We modify one another beyond imagination. Change is imperceptible. Glass is smudged with breath, rain, then broken. This generation remembers the last, but all else is hearsay and wish. What's useless enough to escape notice is born in its own time. What we do without children is artifice; what we do without art is natural. That time won't bend around me indefinitely, that the civilizing cocoon will not last till morning, that meaning will only help me through daylight hours and when night comes will swallow its objects — means I can't sleep. Sleep dances on ahead while the choir chants every failure. My handwriting is harder and harder to read. I invented evolution and now I set stones in the morning dark. Look: Abi and Danny riding off with a string of horses. Listen: a solo frog, wind in grass, a paw on gravel. Listen: nothing.

∾

We are becoming non-human, or non-local, or non-viable, I don't know. And yet.

A misty April morning, branches of new leaves, sky a watery blue, and yet. We can't relinquish the hope of comfort even though storm clouds fester to the west.

∾

One by the river, two by the river.
Which one is kind, which is mean?
One boiling tea, one weaving baskets.

☙

The tent, marginal home, is where the ethnologist unzipped Abi's cut-offs. (I still don't know about James and Danny.) The tent is where she will open her legs for Danny to help her help her baby into the world before the quarry machines engage their gears and dig conglomerate for the next century.

☙

At the beginning of time, at the beginning of our time, just after the first summer, after holidaying in the mountains, valley to valley, picking berries and drinking from wild streams, following our noses, wind filled the trees overnight, replacing leaves with ice, and we took a path by a torrent and found a river and a dry meadow, a coulee of scrub teeming with antelope, and set to work.

☙

There are those who never leave the village, who still linger at the edge of their yards at the end of the growing season to smoke and chatter, family to family, as cool wind blows through leafless orchards and snow begins to drift across the plain from the high peaks. For them the ebb and flow is an ordinary thing — some epochs are restless — and welcomes and questions across the fence are easy. *What of the family? How is your father? How are your cousins?* The to-and-fro paths worn smooth by grandfathers will soon nurse scrub and poplar. Adventure is an interruption of habit, and those who stay expect news from those returning. But they only tell what we can't hear — and to kill time we tame the old epics.

☙

The oral world has faded to a whisper, and written records fall short, end beyond the image after next, just shy of the new word, the new commerce.

～

Yet something calls the way it has always called and this will shape Abi's response to Danny.

We all shrank like this once, after a deep sleep, before light, and called to tomorrow while a tiger roamed close. I caught the habit early and whenever I felt its breath on my neck I took up a pen. In that night-land ghosts and the unborn were indistinguishable from one another.

Now we relinquish time and easy meaning.

27.

They were drawn into the pass at dawn by the almost unwitnessed moment.

She sat staring out, her back against an outcrop. The moon was setting over the hills. Danny had had to carry her. He said she was dilated, the child was knocking her out of her orbit. He pulled down branches and built a fire. He put up the tent, found a mat and a soft blanket and opened a case of tools. He organized and supervised her limbs. He taught her to breathe. He boiled water.

The baby smuggled herself through the crush and slipped out of Abi's womb and the trance was broken. This baby was vigorously curious. After a few moments her fierce look was replaced by a smile.

They heard hawks calling outside.

"I have never seen such perfection," said Danny. "Look. She is already lost in brief things."

∽

On the other side of the pass, they came upon a goat, tall and woolly but terribly thin, wobbling in the scree. As they watched, sitting their sweating horses, Abi side-saddle, the goat bleated at them and turned to scramble away. Its middle, under the wool, was barely a thread, and the effort broke the thread and the creature was in two parts, dead on the ground.

Abi held her baby close and they left the bloodless parts and began their descent through stunted evergreens into a folded land, and were soon in a large valley with divergent paths and tricky streams, scattering herds of healthy goats.

At times they lost each other — the moment the goat died went on in their minds — each trying to hear the other off to the east or west. The ground grew boggy.

"Everything's different," said Abi.

"For sure," said Danny.

"It's a sea change," she said.

"You're right."

"We're doing okay. There's just me and her and you."

"Yes."

"That's something, isn't it?"

"Nothing but. We are blessed."

"Where now?"

"A place where there's plenty of fresh water . . . and fruit. Lots of berries."

∽

The weather changed. A mild wind blew through the valley. The wind opened her so easily! The flight of an arrow or bird, single-minded, no swerve possible. And now the light in the tent, smell of the man, his pain, belonged to her, and these slow days of circling bushes, picking berries, an eye out for bears, was a slow version of flight. She could see every change in the landscape, every shift inside herself, every passing thought. She was not afraid or ashamed. Her baby was content. Something was coming, something she'd need was on its way but not quite here yet. Now they were alive, what they were doing made her feel safe. The rhythm of horse hooves, their own and others. All their breaths and pauses and sleeps and wakenings.

In a way nothing had changed. Yet nothing was the same. They camped on the green land with all the other animals.

∾

Branches waving madly all summer.

"I hurt myself."

"I don't know what you mean, Danny."

"It's just the rock mine."

"You're dreaming, Danny."

"Did you call her Annie?"

"Yes."

∾

Danny opened his eyes and whispered goodnight but the girl was already asleep, on her side with her knees drawn up, in the sleeping bag, her face a disk.

Nights were cold already and he felt they'd made a mistake, putting aside their community. Too late in the year to stay at altitude. He stretched his arms up and pointed his toes to tighten the muscles then let them go loose. Wave of nausea, the horses breathing, a night bird. How long could he control the pain before the pain controlled him?

And he's by a lake with other men watching the girl twist and turn in the water, all skin, light muscle, laughing, showing off, no sign of pregnancy. A complicated feeling, looking at her, seeing her, as the men lift her dripping from the water.

∾

"Abi?"

"Yes?"

"Come over here a moment."

"How are you, Danny?"

"Well, Ms Slip-Slop. Guess what?"

"What?" she asked.

"I'm not so good."

"Your face is white."

"Reminds me I'm living, a lot of pain. Still. How are you, Abi?"

"We're good. Yeah."

"Everything okay?"

"Yeah."

"The horses?"

"Good. Good."

"Annie?"

"She's fine."

"Have you seen the wild ones?"

"No, but I have heard them."

"Just now. I just came through the grape fields. See you there later?"

"Yeah."

∽

"What can I do?"

"As if it is simple. It's too late."

"Danny. What do I do?"

"Well, seems clear to me. We give up or we keep on."

"We keep on. We look after each other."

"What if we can't?"

"We've been here before. Danny, I can't go back."

"I think you should."

"I don't know the way."

"Red does."

～

Sometimes he looked older than anyone she'd seen and other times he was young and beautiful; his illness was unbelievably frightening in its selfishness.

She was beautiful, too, she knew that, but terrible in her protection of Annie.

～

"That doesn't matter."

"What doesn't?"

"It is happening."

"What can I do?"

"Let me look at you is what I'm saying."

"That makes a difference?"

"Your baby won't die."

"I won't let her die."

～

The baby was everything. She couldn't go without food. The horses would get them to the sea. She'd look for signs. A lot to ask, but she had a bit of time.

～

When she woke the sky was light and the man in the tent was snoring. There was frost on her hair. The horses stood tethered, cropping grass and, when she turned over, the baby screamed and she groaned and the horses looked at her and she felt deeply ignorant. She didn't know anything. All she had was this. As she fed Annie, cold surged and she curled up as tight as she could. Afterwards, she lay on her back and stretched. Her belly to the sky, empty as the sky. She pulled her jeans from under her head, unrolled them and struggled them on, stiff and clammy, then slipped out of the sleeping bag.

∼

The greatest time of his life, this. He was in love, and they'd seen the ponies. Six, six. They'd come. They'd come right into the clearing. He was the youngest, stoning the deck, cleaning the shitter, taking the wheel, tying up and casting off. He loved Abi. She was sunburnt and muscular. Annie was his. He was in love. His first time ashore drinking. In front of his eyes the glassy sea — he hadn't loosened the ropes and the tide had gone out, and they were listing. In his ears hoof beats. Not just a headache. On the beach a woman and a dog were running. Drunk, he was sliding off the deck.

He rose on his elbows and looked around. She was gone. He crawled out of the tent. Abi was gone. Red was gone. Annie was gone. All the horses.

∼

Abi spent her second night alone with her baby, awake, looking into Annie's eyes. Back in pandemonium, under an open sky all stars, something churning. A steady flow of tears. Red standing guard. The untethered horses uncertain, questioning.

∼

She was at a loss. The baby had a fever. She felt isolated again, contained, remote. She tied Annie to her front and climbed onto Red. She would ride Red to the pass, through the plain to the vine hills, and then turn right. The others had gone.

28.

What is a story without a happy ending? Through selection is achieved a brief perfection — anticipated — so why dwell on the extinction of things? So much is going on. Abi and Danny in vanishing reveal their grace.

What?

There is something beautiful about them.

What about us, Charles Darwin?

They are beautiful, but you are my life.

Ah, Charles.

The village is my life and you are part of the village.

QED. I've always wanted to prove something. I took Danny's voyages and grew them in a Petri dish. I can't prove he was my brother. Now I'm thin with the telling. Even the best tale will be overlooked in favour of new ones just coming into being. But as long as I am alive *village life is not done*. No, no. No villagers remain, but symbols abound. The stones and the sand might be everything.

The horse-bitten barn sails in all weathers, cracked and missing boards and with holes in the roof. I moved in when Emma died. Everyone but me has left and the village is a collection of low walls and foundations. Long grass grows on the vine hills. The river level changes at random. Summers are often wet and winters bring drought. I remember Emma young, under a tree. We were in love. I remember what she looked like then, perched on a root, hugging her knees, grinning at me.

I might have finished the wall, the path, if there had been enough time. Emma planted honeysuckle for Abi and white clematis for Danny inside the wall, where it could be seen from the glass room. And now the room and house are gone, clematis and yellow honeysuckle are a rampant wave cresting the wall, though there is no inside or outside.

Each winter they wilt and leaves scatter over the sand. Tow-headed weeds grow in the dry ditch in front of the foundations of Tom's house. When it's quiet a hundred Turk's head lilies rattle among the long grasses in the ditch that used to separate his house from the road. I'm used to the perpetual rhythmic roar, imagine machines, imagine waves.

We had a daughter, Emma and I. Annie died when she was ten. It seems as if I have only just found this out, though I've been discovering it all my life.

We had a son who left when he was eighteen and never came home, never wrote. There is parent, child; the space between is empty, waiting. I, thou. Near the beginning, near the end. Light enters through the holes in the roof. Travellers may still return.

I visit Apocat and Kata on the reserve.

"The village," Kata says. "Tell him."

"Ah yes," says Apocat. "A turtle got trapped inside."

"Why was it there?" I ask.

Kata sighs. "Old tribes have brittle bones."

"We held to our own, dear," says Apocat. "Nothing wrong with that."

"Why am I still here?" I ask.

"Yes, that's a puzzle. Is he the projection or the veil? What is he, Kata?"

Kata cackles. "Don't be stupid. That's clear as day."

"I am not needed, Kata."

"Oh, but you are, Charles," says Apocat. "For a little while longer."

"People expect an end, Charles," says Kata.

Strange, the absence of wickedness in the barn. Absence of any emotion, really. I'm just back from my old wall. It's not for dividing anything, you know. It's a promontory. It gives perspective. Look, there's the box-turtle come out from under the straw, lifting his head, craning his neck; he is wary of me, doesn't yet know his life is just some kind of worry. And I hear what he has heard. Over top of the deep explosions, close footfalls: the approach of a horse.